BARKLEY

STRONG MANOR Book 3

KATHI S. BARTON

This is a work of fiction. Names, characters, places, and incidents are products of the author's imagination or are used fictitiously and are not to be construed as real. Any resemblance to actual events, locations, organizations, or persons, living or dead, is entirely coincidental.

World Castle Publishing, LLC
Pensacola, Florida

Copyright © 2023 Kathi S. Barton
Paperback ISBN: 9798891260061
eBook ISBN: 9798891260078
First Edition World Castle Publishing, LLC, June 25, 2023
http://www.worldcastlepublishing.com

Licensing Notes

Cover: Karen Fuller
Editor: Karen Fuller

Chapter 1

Barkley watched the people in the mall. He didn't come there often, but he'd been close to the place when he decided he was starving and couldn't wait the extra thirty minutes to get home and fix himself something to fill the void. So now that he was finished eating, he just watched the people while keeping an eye on his laptop for news from a couple of firms and people that he was finding out if they'd sell to them. And at a reasonable price. He was always in the market for a floundering company to restructure. In the end, everyone benefited from the deal.

He liked to people-watch and noticed that most of the people walking around were women. For the most part, today, the place was nearly empty. Most of the women there today were fairly young. Some had small children with them, from about the age of four down. Infants, too, in strollers that more than likely cost more than his first car. But what boggled his mind the most was that about eighty percent of the mothers or nannies, he supposed it could be, were carrying the babies and piling their purchases into the infant's seat. He just didn't understand people nowadays.

Looking down at his laptop when it dinged that an email was dropped into his box, he pulled it up just as shouting down by one of the anchor stores began. It wasn't just shouting, but the two women were using language he'd not heard since he'd been in college. Boy, oh boy, they were both pissed off about something. He had a very scary thought about the two strollers that were near each woman as they screamed something about clothing and a sale.

Opening the email, he thought about how angry people seemed to be about the dumbest things nowadays. He supposed there was reason for it. Money was tight everywhere. People were being laid off right and left. And children, older married kids were moving back home to save money on necessities such as food, transportation as well as just being able to take care of their children. He read the email twice before he realized this person was serious.

"Since we both know you and your family have more money than sense, I'm going to need four million dollars for my place. That way, I can get me something out of the deal after having had to wait on my mother to die so that I can have it. I don't want it, you understand. But if I'm going to sell it, I want to get as much as you'll give me." He laughed before starting a response to the man. The fight at the other end of the mall, however, had him putting away his things and heading to the closest restaurant that was still open.

The gun firing off had both women down on the floor surprised him. The older woman had pulled her gun out from under her shirt and just fired at the purple-haired one. The people who had been watching what was going on scattered, heading to the doors. He watched as all the stores at that end of the mall closed up their heavy sliding doors. Barkley knew for a fact it was an automated thing that had been recently put into service. Barton had been working on the design with Jade since she'd told him how much it would save in the long run for stores.

People were rushing by him to get out of the mall. Not that he blamed them, as one of the women stood up with their firearm still in their hand and pointed it at the woman still on the floor. Barkley shoved all his things into his briefcase and handed it over to the restaurant that was closest to him for safekeeping.

"Call the police." The kid just stared at him. "Wake up, damn it. Call the police and tell them there has been a shooting at the mall. Do it now!"

The kid, because he couldn't have been much more than sixteen, finally got over the shock of what was going on not ten feet from him and closed the doors to the little place. The manager, someone he thought he knew, told him he'd put his things in the office and it would be locked up.

"Good. Get out of here. And make sure you pass it along to others to get out as well. And to lock the door behind you, only letting the police in when they arrive. You can do that, right?" Nodding, the man called the police as Barkley was making his way to the two women. He was terrified out of his mind but more afraid for the two strollers that did have children in them around the two women. The babies were screaming loudly, no doubt terrified of the yelling and the gun going off so close to them. Barkley hoped that neither of them had been shot or injured when the gun had been fired.

He got their attention by whistling. Loud and long that he'd perfected over the years with five brothers in the house. They both looked at him. "I could care less right now if you kill each other. But there is no reason those children should be harmed in the process. If you'll allow me to take them to—"

"Stay the fuck away from my grandkids." He nodded, putting his hands up when he was told to do so. "You're not the fucking police. Why are you even here? Mind your own business."

"I was until you two started up. The police have been called and are on their way." He heard the sirens just as he finished telling the blond woman, the one who had claimed that the babies were her grandchildren. "Hear them? They're not going to be very happy when they get here."

Barkley looked at the other woman. Her hair was

bright purple, and it didn't suit her skin tone at all, he thought. It washed her out until she was almost clear with it. However, it occurred to him then it could have been from loss of blood. But it soon wouldn't matter to anyone what color she had her hair dyed. Because the way she was losing blood while sitting back down on the floor meant she wasn't going to make it to the hospital, no matter what sort of tricks the medic's tired.

"This is all her fault. If she'd just backed off when I told her to move, I could have gotten the little dresses I wanted before her. She took them all. She started this. I don't understand one bit why my son went and married her. She's useless." Barkley wanted to ask her if prison was something she was willing to go to rather than have a dress on sale. But he didn't. He wasn't stupid. "You tell the police when they get here you saw the whole thing, and it was her fault. Or I might just shoot you too."

"I didn't see anything. Just heard you two shouting at each other." The police announced that they wanted Blond to put down her gun. Barkley didn't move when he heard them coming up behind him. But he did tell them what was going on when asked. "This woman here killed the other woman that's on the floor. They're in-laws to each other. The son is married, I guess, to the purple-haired woman. If she's not already dead, then she will be soon enough. I only came here to see if I could get the babies out of harm's way."

Purple had fallen back on the floor. He couldn't tell if she was still breathing or not, but then he wasn't a doctor. The police told Blond to drop the gun, and she fired at the cop standing next to him, and that was all it took to have the other officers open fire on her. It was going to be difficult, he thought as he sat down on the floor to determine which bullet had killed the older woman. It looked as if they'd emptied their clips into her head and chest.

Barkley held the two babies in his arms, keeping them entertained while the police were doing whatever was needed to make the scene clear. He'd been asked by Officer Buddy Morgan to see if he could get the little girls to calm down. All he'd done was sit on the floor when they were handed to him, and they quieted right up.

The mall had been pretty much emptied before the police had arrived, and now they were waiting on the coroner to make his decision on what was the cause of death of the two women. Not that it wasn't obvious. Morgan told him they were doing this by the books so that when it went to trial, it was over with the first time. The entire thing was being recorded, and he was glad the mall manager had turned over all the camera footage as soon as it had been asked for.

"Barkley, are you sure you're all right?" He said he was fine and he'd not been hurt. He also told the officer, someone he'd gone to school with, that he'd only been trying to get the little ones out of the way. "Yes, the cameras show that you only happened on the scene when the daughter-in-law was shot."

He'd realized the two women were related, and he could tell the babies were twins. Barkley was one himself and enjoyed watching over the children until the right people came to pick them up. Barkley had been told the daughter-in-law didn't get along with her mother-in-law from the start. Now they were both dead, and the younger woman's husband was on his way to the mall now to talk to the police. Jade showed up just as the husband did.

"I'm here to make sure you're all okay." He

said he'd told them several times that he was. "Yes, but Buddy over there, he said that he knows you, said that shock might make you not feel any pain for hours. I don't see any blood, so I'm assuming he's a worry wart."

"Yes, that's his first name. I couldn't remember. But I'm fine. However, this little girl seems to be too fussy. Not that I know a great deal about babies, but she's nothing like her sister. I can't seem to be able to put her in any position that she seems comfortable in." Taking the little girl from him, Mick, the girl's father, came to ask if he could hold them. "The police said to wait until they were examined. Then you can hold them until they take them to the hospital. They want to check them out, I guess."

Mick watched as Jade stripped the little girl — Mick said her name was Sunny — down to her bare skin. Finding bruises all over her legs and arms alarmed them all. Jade asked Mick if he could explain the reason for them. They were in different stages of healing, and the most recent ones looked to be about two hours old.

"I don't know. I mean, my mom, she watches the girls from time to time. She had them both last night. But I'm working on-site in Virginia now and only arrived home an hour ago. I didn't even know they were meeting here today. This place is a good hour from where we live." Buddy Morgan was taking notes and asked for his boss's name and number. After giving it to him, Mick cried. "She, my mother, beat me as a child. But since the girls have been born, she seemed to have changed a great deal. We didn't use her as a sitter all that often, but the girls, even for as young as they are, never seemed to mind her holding them. Christ, my wife is gone. What am I going to do now?"

Jade didn't speak to the man, but she did want to make sure the other little girl, Bethany, wasn't bruised as well. But the fact of the matter was, there seemed to be more on her than on Sunny. Instead of allowing Mick to hold his daughters, he was told that they'd have to be taken to the hospital for x-rays as well as a full work up. Mick was so over the top upset that Barkley was having a hard time believing that he didn't know what was going on with his own children. Even being away from home as much as he claimed, it bothered him that he'd not noticed what was going on.

He certainly would have.

 After the children were taken by ambulance to the hospital, Jade sat with him on the floor. He didn't say anything to her about what had happened, nor did he tell her what he was thinking. But when she asked him his opinion, he couldn't help but let her know his feelings about the dad.

 "I mean, even though I don't have any knowledge of babies, I knew that one of them was in pain or at least upset about me holding her. I didn't undress her, well, because that would just make me a target on all kinds of levels I don't want to have to deal with. Anyway. What do you think?" She said she'd felt the same thing. That even she noticed the children were more happy being with a stranger than they wanted to be with their own father. "I didn't think about that. But you're right. Neither of them reached out for him when he showed up. Like they didn't want their own father to comfort them."

 "It's something I see quite often, I'm afraid. But the hospital personal will look into things. I mentioned it to the medics when I followed them out with the children. Hopefully, I get to kick some asses to get them to see what the larger picture is." An elderly man showed up just as the bodies of the two women were being taken away. He only had eyes for his son and no one else. He didn't ask after the babies either, or the women for that matter. "This is going to be a tell-tale meeting. A thought just occurred to me that he got here fairly quickly for a man who lives an hour away. That is what he said, right?"

He hadn't any idea what she meant until the father came up to his son and spoke. Not loud, but loud enough for him and Jade to hear what he said as they were that close to them.

"Don't worry, son. It's going to be just fine now that they're both going to be blamed for what happened to the girls." Mick told his dad that his mom had killed his wife. "That's fine too, right? Now we have them, and the girls will be just ours now."

Jade didn't say a word but looked at the officers that were with the medical examiner right now. Barkley didn't know what was going on yet, but he was sure it was something huge. And he'd bet anything that this 'incident' that had happened today had been planned out. Perhaps not that the wife of the man being killed, but it seemed to be all right with the two of them that it had happened for some reason that sent shivers down his spine.

~*~

"Carrie, there's a phone call for you. Something about your sister." She told her secretary to take a message. "It's the police, honey. They said they can only speak to you."

"Christ." Punching in the numbered line the call was on, Carrie barked out her name and told the person on the other end she wasn't going to bail her sister out, no matter if she only needed money for a ticket. "Also, tell Matty that since she married the fucking prick, then she's going to have to deal with whatever has happened to her. I'm not going to get caught up in her drama again."

"I'm sorry to tell you this, Ms. Boone, but Madeline Cartwright was killed yesterday evening by her mother-in-law, Jane Cartwright. Who was then killed by the police when she wouldn't put her gun down." Well, that was nothing she expected, and she told the man that. "I thought not. Right now, the babies, you did know she had a set of twin girls, didn't you?

They're in protective custody."

"I had no idea, to be honest with you, that she was still alive." He didn't say anything, for which she was grateful. She thought that she sounded cold and heartless. But she couldn't deal with this. Not anymore. "Look, Mr. Strong. I can't help you out with anything, including the babies. My sister parted ways with us a long time ago, and we've not spoken in…let me think. At least fifteen years. I can't raise her children or even take them in. I just can't. If you've been able to find me, you've more than likely found out Mattie has four brothers. They're not going to help with them either. You can ask them if you want, but I know they're going to tell you they can't do it either. Mattie is…was a handful when we were children, and she burnt all her bridges and used up all the goodwill she might well have had from us a long time ago. Thank you for informing me of her death. But I'm sorry. I won't be able to help."

Putting the phone back in the cradle, she sat there for a while, thinking of her last conversation with Mattie. It really had been fifteen years ago. Carrie herself had only been ten or eleven at the time when

Mattie had had her arrested along with her parents. She claimed that they'd had her chained up in the basement of the home and had starved her over the last six months.

While she was in jail on those trumped-up charges about abusing her older sister, Mattie had gone through the family home and stolen everything of any value. Including Mom and Dad's social security check, their bank card and credit cards. It wasn't until they got out that they saw what they'd lost.

Picking up the phone again, she called Robert. He wasn't working today, so she knew she had a fifty-fifty chance of getting in touch with him. His life partner answered on the first ring.

"Hello, my lovely. What can I do for you today?" She asked if Robert was home. "No. He's gone to the — what's happened? You sound very upset." She told him everything.

"I don't know what the guy wanted for me to do. I didn't ask him, but I'm not going to take on her issues anymore. She hasn't been a part of our lives forever, it seems." Dan agreed with her. "I'm going to call the others and let them know what is going on. Could you please tell Robert for me? You'd more than likely be nicer than I'd be telling him that she's gone."

"I will. But I can almost guarantee you he won't want anything to do with—did he tell you she called here about five months ago? She wanted money, of course, and said that he had to pay her for all the pain and suffering she had to go through being a sister to a faggot. I kid you not, Carrie. I thought he was going to blow a gasket. But all he did was hang up, and he asked me to have our number changed. I did that the very next day." She asked why he hadn't told her. "You have your own demons about Mattie, honey. I'm sure that was the only reason he didn't tell you. But it's all water under the bridge now, and we're going to keep going the way that we were before. She's not been a part of our lives for so long. We've gone on without her. Right?"

"Right." She didn't feel bad about her sister dying, not even the way that she had died. It had been too long, as Dan said. Carrie pulled out her cell phone and called the others. None of them, as she had predicted, wanted anything to do with Mattie. Not after all that she'd done to all of them over the years.

Going back to work, she was just finishing up for the day when Robert called her back. He wasn't upset either but invited her over for dinner. Any chance she had at not having to cook for herself or go out to eat was something she would jump on. Telling him she'd be there in twenty minutes. She was just leaving the office when her phone rang again. She didn't know the number that came up and almost didn't answer it. When she did, she had to sit down on the floor.

"This is Mick Cartwright, your dead sister's husband. I need to make a few things clear to you. Are you coming here to try and take my precious daughters from me?" She asked him what he was talking about. "My daughters. I'm sure you've been notified by now that Mattie is dead. My mom is too. Stupid cow. Sunny and Bethany are staying with me. I'm their father, and you'll keep away from us. Do I make myself clear?"

"As mud. Why would I want to have anything to do with my *dead sisters*, as you put it, kids when I'd had nothing to do with her long before you were in the picture." He laughed and told her she'd better be thinking that way forever. They were his daughters. "So you keep pointing out. Why is that, I wonder?"

Pulling out her cell phone, she messaged Robert, telling him to just listen in on the conversation. Then she called him to have him listen too. As Mick went on and on about how he was going to be raising his daughters, she had a feeling that there was something off about him and the conversation.

He spoke to her for another thirty minutes. Mostly it was to threaten her about coming around, but he also made it a point to tell her, several times, that he and his father were going to raise the twins and there wasn't anything she could do about it. Again, she had an eerie feeling he was trying hard to brag to her about something, and it was up to her to guess what that might be.

"I'm going to have her cremated too. That way, there isn't going to be exhuming her body later down the line when you or your brothers get a burr up your asses about something and try and sue me. I've won." She told him congratulations. "You bet your sweet ass it's going to be congratulations all around for me once I get her insurance money."

"I'm assuming this was all planned? That my sister was to die at your mother's hands, and you'd get to collect on both their policies that you just happened to have taken out a few months ago?" She sat at her deck and looked up the name Strong. The man who had called her to let her know that Mattie was dead. She had to ask what Mick said when she realized he was probably waiting on an answer from him. "Well, did you? Take out the policy just to have your mom kill her?"

"I guess we'll never know. And I hadn't expected my mother to be killed. It's a shame but nothing that we can't overcome." She asked him what that was supposed to mean. "Well, I'll tell you this, it's going to mean that we have to find us someone we can trust to watch over my daughters while Dad and I make plans for them."

The most profound feeling of sickness rolled over her. While he didn't come right out and say it—and hopefully, she was wrong—but it sounded to her like he was going to be selling off his daughters to anyone with the right amount of money to have them. They were just babies.

Finding the newspaper article, just a few lines about a mall shooting, had her thinking that it was about Mattie. As she and Mick spoke, mostly him doing the bragging about shit, she found the name of a Strong family nearby. Looking up his phone number with the tools she had at her disposal, she also found a phone number and address for the Strong Foundation. Taking a chance, she emailed a plea for someone to call her back in about an hour. She needed desperately to talk to someone about her sister's husband and daughters.

Putting her phone back in the cradle again, she sat there for several minutes thinking about the shit he'd said to her. When her cell rang, she was glad to see the face of Robert there. The first words out of his mouth were that he'd recorded every word of what was said between her and Mick.

"Thank you for that. I'm going to have to talk to this Strong guy that called me this morning. Also, I'd like to be able to get in touch with the insurance company that is holding the policy on Mattie." Robert asked her if she could do that, find the policy. "Yes. I mean, that's what I do. Find information on insurance policies and determine if they are bogus or not. Do you suppose they lived in the little town that the shooting happened in?"

As she did her research, Robert told her he was going to look into something as well. That he'd call her back in a bit. While still searching for where the policy might be held by, her cell phone rang again. It was the same number that had called her earlier that had started all this.

Without waiting for the person on the other end to speak, she launched into her feelings that she'd had about Mick. She also asked him if he possibly knew who the insurance company was so she could put a hold on that.

"Also, he told me he's having Mattie cremated, so I couldn't come back later and have her exhumed for whatever reason. I'm not sure what he thinks I'd do that for, but now that's all I want to do. Or am I too late to have her get a full autopsy?" The man laughed, and she felt stupid, which, as usual, flared up her temper. "Listen here, you bastard. I was doing just fine in my life, not having a clue about what Mattie was up to or, as I said, even if she was alive. She was the most horrific person I know — knew. Now that you've opened up this can of worms, you're going to be helping me out so that whatever plans that idiot has for those children, I can put a stop to. I'm serious here when I tell you that I think he's going to be selling them off for sex to perverts. And if he does that, I'm going to kill him myself."

"I agree." She'd not expected that and told the man that. "I know. You seemed to have a full head of steam going as soon as you answered. And I do have answers, or at least partial answers, for some of your concerns. Mattie hasn't been cremated as yet. Her body and that of Mick's mother are being put on hold until the state can bring in a person to do the autopsy on them. Nothing will be done to them until that time. Also, the girls are in protective custody. He made some odd comments around the police that had them keeping him away from the girls for the present time. Also, you'll be happy to know he's already tried to cash in the policy on her but can't without a death certificate. Could be another reason he wants her cremated so quickly."

"I'm an insurance investigator. If you can tell me the name on the policy, I can get more information on it than you can." After he told her the company and the policy number his dad had found, she started to work immediately. "It's for one million dollars. I'm betting if you have a look around like I'm doing right now — bingo. He has seven policies on Mattie worth a million each. And he's the benefactor on all of them. However, there isn't one on him. I guess he plans on never dying. All right. Let me dig a little deeper here and find out about his mother. Yes, the same thing. One million with each of the seven policies. Also, there are none on his father. Which to me it's a giant red flag."

Her desk phone rang, and she answered it. Robert told her he'd found a few things. Telling Mr. Strong that she was going to put him on speaker phone with her brother and her, Robert started telling them what he'd been able to find out.

"There are several records of the little girls being in and out of the hospital emergency room over their lifetime. The first one was when they were two weeks old, and Sunny suffered a broken arm. Mattie told them that she'd been picking her up in the middle of the night and had dropped her on the bed railing. They must have believed her because there isn't any record of a police report filed. It happened again, a burnt hand for Bethany when she was flaying her hands around and touched her too-hot coffee. That was investigated as well, but no arrests were made. There are a few for Mattie, too, but nothing like the girls." Mr. Strong asked about the mother-in-law. "Hang on a minute. I can pull that up right now since I'm already in the system. Yes. I have fifteen times where she was brought into the hospital by ambulance over the last twelve months. The husband or her son would go and get her, take her home, and there wasn't any follow-up made to any local doctors. Let me see here. Broken leg. Broken jaw. There is also a couple of times when she was unconscious when she was found. Blunt trauma is what I'm seeing here. Again, she didn't stay any longer than it took for one of the others to come and get her out."

"What is it you do, Robert? Carrie said she is an insurance investigator. You have to be something similar to that." Robert told him what it was he did. "So you've gotten into the hospital system and gotten what you need. I don't think that is legal."

"Depends, I suppose. Neither is trying to kill off your wife or sister. Nor selling off six-month-old babies to perverts. I do what I do in order to help Carrie with her job. It pays well, and I have no reason to leave the house unless I want to. If you have a problem with me and—"

"No. No, I'm sorry if I gave that impression. What you're doing for this case, and I'm thinking that it's going to have to be taken before a judge sooner rather than later, is going to be a great deal of help keeping the little girls safe." Robert thanked him. "No worries there. But I do have to ask again. Will any of you be coming here to help out with your sister's murder? If for no other reason than to help the children of her be safe?"

"I'll be there on the next flight out. That is if you're accepting of my husband being with me." Mr. Strong said he didn't care who he was partnered with so long as they could get to the bottom of this. "Carrie? You're going as well, aren't you?"

"Yes. I'll be there. If for no other reason than to see Mick put in jail for the rest of his life." She didn't want to ask but needed to know. "I'm assuming the children were examined by a doctor. Have they been sexually abused?"

"Yes." Nothing more was needed than that answer to have her hurting for them. "I'll wait to hear from the two of you when you're arriving and have a place for you to stay. We'll get this prick."

After they all hung up, she sat at her desk for a few minutes just to think about what had happened to those babies. Then it occurred to her that Mattie more than likely knew it. She had to. And that made her hurt all the more for those two little girls.

Chapter 2

Mick didn't care for waiting his turn. He never had, even as a child. But today, he had been told to be on his best behavior or else. He knew well enough not to ask his dad what he meant by that. The shit would be knocked out of him, and he'd be in the fucking vet's office again recovering.

The vet that they'd been using for the last few years also knew better than to say a word about what he was doing behind closed doors. The man had gotten rid of so many bodies for them over the course of the last ten years. Having to cut the dead up so they'd fit in his crematorium wasn't all that bad when he thought about it. Mess? Hell yeah. But there wasn't a single bit of the body left but some ash that went out with all the little doggies that had kicked the bucket too. He did oftentimes wonder if people wondered why their little bitty dog had so much ash in his jar. Laughing at what their faces might look like if they found out was funny to him.

"Mr. Cartwright, the attorney will see you now." This was the fourth attorney he'd seen today about getting the county medical examiner to release Mattie's body. As he stood up with his file in hand, he looked at the woman who had summoned him just now. She hurried behind her desk when he asked her out. "No. Didn't your wife just die, sir? I'd think you'd be mourning her rather than hitting on someone else already."

"I just need some comfort, you know? A little fucking around with you could go a long way in making me feel better." She didn't say a word to him, which, as usual, he took as a nod for him to keep at her until he got his way. However, before he could tell her how good he was in the sack, the attorney called to him from the office he'd been headed to. "We'll talk later. I promise."

He was in the office when he realized that there were too many people in the room for him to be having a private visit with the man. Not that he could remember his name, but something was amiss, as his dad would say. Sitting down when he was asked to have a seat, he waited on them to make the first move.

"Mr. Cartwright, you've come to see about getting your wife's body released to you. Is that correct?" He said they'd had her long enough that he wanted her in her resting place. "Yes. I have that on the notes here. You also said that you wanted no autopsy done nor anything taken from her body, such as tissue samples and blood. Is that also correct?"

"It is. I want her to be cremated like she came into this world. With everything where it belongs." His dad had come up with that before Mattie had been killed. "She was my wife of six years, and I would know her better than anyone else on that matter. I think…no, I know she would have been sorely upset to know someone had tampered with her body before she was cremated."

"Why cremation?" He didn't know the woman who asked though he thought he should have. "Doctor

Jade Strong. I was at the mall the day your wife and mother were killed. Why are you having her cremated? According to what we've been able to find out about your wife, she never mentioned that was her plan to any of her friends."

"My wife didn't spread her personal information around like most would." He had no idea why, but this woman was making him very nervous. Sitting on his hands so that he'd not be giving away any telltale information, he smiled. "Mattie also said that she didn't want to linger in a vegetable state either."

"It's a vegetative state. According to her diary that she had on her when she was murdered, she was fearful of something happening to her that you would have been involved in. She left numbers for the police to call if something did happen to her. She also detailed how the two of you were not getting along and she was afraid for her daughters. What do you think she meant by that?" He didn't know but was afraid to open his mouth to make anything up. "No answer? All right. As you know, her daughters are in protective custody. Do you know why?" He said he had no idea why he wasn't able to have his precious babies back. "They've been sexually abused. Also beaten and burned with what appears to be a—"

"It's all Mattie's doing." He felt the air in his lung refuse to exhale, and he was getting a little dizzy from it. "Mattie was an abusive person. She had men at the house all the time when I was working."

He was off script, and he knew that he was just a few more sentences away from getting himself into deeper trouble. Closing his mouth, biting his lips hard enough he could taste blood, he stared at the woman who was messing things up for him.

Mick wanted his dad. He needed him to tell him what to say, what to do. But as it stood right now, he thought that keeping his mouth shut, no matter what they asked him about, was his best bet. Taking a few calming breaths, he looked at the woman again when she asked him if he was afraid.

"Afraid? Of what? I've done nothing wrong." Not that they knew about anyway. "I just came in here to see about getting Mattie's body released so I can move on with my life. I think I've made it perfectly clear what I want to be done, and these accusations that you're saying to me are making me think you're going to try and blame whatever happened to my wife on me."

"No. We're only going to try and get you to confess to abusing your daughters." The look the attorney gave him when he spoke made the sweat he was feeling running down his spine start to feel like a waterfall. He wanted to get up and leave, but he wasn't sure that his legs would carry him very far. Mick was afraid. Terrified really. While he didn't know how they'd come to know so much, he was sure that if he could just get out of there, he'd be all right. "Your home, the one you shared with your wife and daughters, has been locked from your being able to enter. Your father's home has been as well. There are just too many holes in the story that we're getting from the two of you about what happened to the two women and your daughters."

"I want my daughters." The attorney told him that, for now, it wasn't going to happen. "Why not? I'm their father. I should be with them now that they've lost their mother."

"Regardless of your relationship to them, you're not going to see them until such time as the courts deem you fit to be their guardian." He stood up and sat down when a man about the size of a car told him to sit down. The attorney continued. "Your credit cards have all been closed off from you being able to use them as well. Your bank account has been frozen as well, as your passport and other credentials have been confiscated."

He didn't know what to do. Mick tried to think what his father would have done and laughed. Dad would laugh and pretend to blow things off like it meant little to nothing to him. Even though they could see the sweat stains on his shirt, he tried for the bravo behavior.

"Like I care what you cut off. I have money on me now that I could survive whatever. Since I know I didn't do a thing wrong." He thought about what had been said to him. "You know, I only came in here to cash in my insurance policy. It's you all that have been treating me like I've done something wrong. What is wrong with you guys? Can't a man get his money coming to him to provide for his children?"

Mick particularly liked that part of his speech. Providing for his children. When he knew that it was his children that were going to be providing for him. Not that he was keen on them being sold off the way his father had imagined.

His mother had been sitting for the girls when they'd been about six weeks old. Going to pick them up when Mattie was in a particularly bad way after he'd had a bit of fun with her, he saw that they were bleeding when he went to change their diapers before leaving. Screaming at his mom, trying to find out what she'd done to them, he finally got an answer that, to this day, sent chills down his spine when he thought about it.

"Oh, your father did that. It's no big deal, Micky. He was only having a bit of fun with them. Just like he did with you when you were that age. It's all right." But it wasn't all right. Not even now did he think it was completely all right with him. But his father had told him he was going to do it, and he'd had no choice. Mick was terrified of his dad. Had always been. "You won't be repeating this to anyone, Micky dear. If you do, you know your dad will bring a hell down on your head that you'll never live with. He'll kill you."

"They're babies," Mick had told her. "Mom,

they're only babies. Why would he do something like that to his own granddaughters?"

She shrugged before answering him. "I don't know why he does a lot of things he does, Micky. Just shut your mouth and take them home. Or not. If you leave them here for a bit, perhaps you can get on your father's good side again."

Mick didn't take the girls over there for two months after that. He figured that, sadly, if they were older, then he'd be not interested in them anymore. But as it turned out, his father was happy with them no matter their age. Mick went home that night after dropping the girls off at his moms, sick to his stomach. Not only that, but he was tempted to go to the police, but what his father said to him as he was leaving was still ringing in his ears.

"You do anything stupider, Micky and I'll make you pay for it. I'm not above killing you and that wife of yours for what I want. You understand that, don't you?" He nodded and started to tell his dad that they were just babies. "You go on home now and keep that trap of yours shut. Otherwise, they'll be finding you and Mattie dead in your beds, then who do you think will have them babies? All the time too. Go on home."

He had. And since then, he'd not turned his father down once when he called for his granddaughters. Being afraid of his father was something he thought most people would be if they had to spend any time with him. Or, for that matter, talked to anyone that had had to deal with him on a one on one basis. Michael Cartwright was a man that all should be afraid of if they had half a brain.

Leaving the attorney's office, not accomplishing a thing, he headed to his car. When he was seated inside of it, he watched as his father's entourage pulled up in front of the bank across the street from him. Mick nearly got out of his car and waved at his father, but something held him back. When he looked in his direction, Mick even ducked down behind the dashboard to hide. Something that he'd never done in his life concerning his father.

Sitting there, without much in the way of thought as to what he was doing, Mick pulled his phone out of his pocket and looked at the pictures he had of Bethany and Sunny. Christ, they were beautiful little girls. Sliding through them one after another, he got to one of his mom holding them. Then the next one was of his father. Mick, sick to his stomach again, opened his car door and threw up the breakfast he'd had this morning.

Getting seated again, Mick made his way out of town. He had a second place that he could call home for a while, but he bypassed that place as well. Nearly to Columbus, about twenty minutes away, he pulled over to the side of the road and sat there. Reaching into the glove box, knowing he had no other choice than what was before him, Mick pulled out the revolver that he'd had for the last few months and held it in his hand as he sat there sobbing about how shitty his life had become.

~*~

Carrie got off the plane and stomped all the way to the luggage area. She was going to kill each of her brothers before they ever got to see Mr. Strong. Why they had insisted on coming here with her, she had no idea. And had told them that several times on the way here. When she saw the sign with her last name on it, the man holding it up was laughing. She didn't care for that either.

"What the hell do you find so funny? Or are you addled? You'd have to be if you think that this is going to end in any way other than the one I told you it would." He said he was laughing at her, who he assumed were her brothers trying to catch up with her. "Yeah. They're idiots. I've been on my own for a long time, and they think that I need them to come here with me to protect me." They'd caught up with her by then.

"Protect you? I would imagine you have absolutely no trouble protecting yourself. Them too if it came down to it." Robert laughed as he agreed with him. "I'm Barkley Strong. My father is the attorney who is going to be helping the five of you. My parents and family are at their home working on the information that they've found so far. Also, my brother Jenson. He's running for Congress right now, so he doesn't have a great deal of time, but he is willing to help all of you."

"Thank you all for that. We really did come to protect Carrie but not in the way you might think. We'll be there to keep her out of trouble." She told her older brother to fuck off. "Thank you, sweetheart. I love you too. This is all the luggage we brought with us. While we didn't know how long this was going to take, we did bring things to go to court." Robert smiled at Barkley and introduced the others to him. "We thought it would be a good show of force to come here and be there for the girls. While, as you've been told, we didn't know our sister all that well, we will fight for her daughters. Have you heard any more from their father?"

"He is trying to cash in the policies he had on his wife and mother." Carrie asked how many he had as they were loading into the stretch limo that seemed to perfectly time pulling up in front of the airport for them. Barkley told her they'd found seven so far. "Christ, what an idiot. You know that's a red flag in my line of work. I'm assuming, too, that his father has done the same thing?"

"You'd be correct." Barkley, a large man, sat across from her. "Michael, the older Cartwright, is a big name around town. Not in a particularly good way, either. He's a bully, and from what we've been able to unearth about him, he gets what he wants no matter if he has to take out a couple of people to get it. Not that we have proof of him murdering anyone. But there have been a few missing people he's had trouble with."

"Where are the girls?" Barkley told her that they were at his brother's home with twenty-four/seven care. "I'm assuming that that's for a good reason too."

"Yes. So nothing comes back on us about their condition when they were placed in his home. Bethany is having the hardest time adjusting to her new home. Not that she's being bad or anything like that. But I believe that she's still in a great deal of pain from the cuts and bruises on her little body. Sunny? Well, she's just as her name implies she is. Happy. Smiling and cooing. My mother said that Bethany acts like she isn't interested in what's going on around her, but when she hears her sister laugh, she does look for her." It was Andrew that asked how badly the girls had suffered. He was handed a thick file. "Both of them have been sexually abused, as we told you before you came out. Between them, they've had seven broken ribs and three broken arms as well as Bethany has had some stitches in her backside from being whipped with something. Jade, my sister-in-law, is a doctor, and she said it looked as if she'd been whipped with a leather strap. Those are healing well now that she has good care."

Carrie shivered. To think that they'd gone through all that and still came out on top. Because she was going to make sure that her brother-in-law and his dad paid for what they'd done to them. She'd been telling her brothers that she hoped that Mattie is rotting in her grave if she was aware of what was going on with them. She said that to Barkley.

"There isn't any way that she didn't know. Or wasn't aware of it. Twice she brought the girls to the emergency department for bleeding. We're still looking for the full records for that. There is a video of her bringing them into the hospital, but there is no one noted as treating them. Then four hours later, there is a video of her taking them out of the hospital. Dad thinks that Michael had something, if not all, to do with that. Also, we've found out that Mick, he is abused as well, goes to the local vet when he's been hurt."

This was far worse than she thought it was going to be. She had two nieces that she'd never met that were hurt in ways that no one, not at any age less than eighteen years old, to be hurt. And by their own blood. It made her blind with rage when she thought of the things that had been done to them in the name of love.

While the others talked, she turned to look out the window. She needed to tune things out for a little bit. Carrie didn't think she could take much more information today. For the last four days, since the first call about Mattie, it's all she'd thought about, dreamed about and talked about with her family. She thought about the conversation that she'd had with CarolAnn, Andrew's wife.

"Don't hold the babies if you're not going to be bringing them back with you. That's all it will take." Carrie told her that she wasn't going to, no matter what she did with them. "You'll need them in your life if you so much as smell them, Nat. I swear. They have some kind of chemical stuff going on when they're born to make a person stupid when they touch them. I was like that too."

"Are you telling me not to touch them or not to smell them? Because either one of those I do or not do is going to have them looking at me like a cold and heartless aunt." CarolAnn just stared at her. "I'm not cold and heartless."

"No. You're not. But you remember when Jack was born? How you avoided coming over for months, so you'd not have to be around him?" Carrie said it wasn't the same. "It most certainly is the same. The moment he reached for you from my arms, no less, you took him into your heart. And you love him as much, if not more, than I do."

"He's a special kid." She told her that they were all special. "Not like Jack is. He's a great kid and loves me no matter if I bring him gifts or not."

"You forever bring him gifts. And if you're not bringing them, you're having them shipped to him. You're a good aunt but a sap too." Carrie told her that she wasn't being fair. "I'm being realistic. If you get to see them, even from a distance, you'll be sucked in like the rest of us will be. In fact, that's the reason that none of the women of this family wanted to go. We'd be packing them off to our homes before the ink was dry on adoption papers."

"I can't raise them, CarolAnn. I know nothing about babies and what they might need. I don't know how to love anyone but you guys." She told her that she'd find a man and he'd make everything perfect for her. "There isn't anyone out there like that. Not for me. Not that I'm looking, either. I don't want to have to be attached to someone that will hurt me."

"Not everyone is like Randal, honey. You do know that, don't you?" She nodded, her heart broken again for what had been done to her. "Carrie, honey, don't let one asshole make you not try to love again. If you do, then your loss will be overwhelming."

"I'm not closing off my heart to anyone." CarolAnn just stared at her. "All right, I am, but I'll be all right. I'm much too caustic for anyone to want to get near me anymore anyway. And I think that I like that—"

The limo had stopped. She hadn't any idea when but she knew that it had been a while. Her brothers were out, and she was sitting there with Barkley, who was on his cell phone. The door was open to the car, and she could see her brothers. She did wonder why they'd not poked her or something. Carrie looked at Barkley when he said her name.

"Are you all right?" She said that she wasn't sure anymore. "Yeah, I get that. It's going to be all right. My family, along with yours, is working hard to make sure that the two of them pay. And they will too."

"I don't know if I believe you or not. Not you,

but believe in justice anymore." She looked out the window and then back to him before continuing. "I'm jaded, I'll admit to that. Things in my personal life as well as professional life, have made me that way. I don't trust easily. I certainly don't lean on many people, even when I probably should. People, my sister included, are mean, selfish people that only have their best interests in mind when they plot and plan things that they know aren't right."

"What is it you do?" She told him. "That's right. I remember you telling me that on the phone. I can see where that would have you jaded. Even having as limited idea of what your job would entail, I can see where people would be pissy with you about denying their claims. Like this case with the Cartwrights. I'm sure you see this all the time."

"I do. More than I think people realized it." Barkley asked if she'd been able to look over the policy that was on her sister. "I have. He will get double the payout if she was murdered. Not that there is any doubt that she was murdered, but if he had anything at all to do with her demise, he'll get nothing. I think that's why he wants her cremated so badly."

"My dad, he's looking into the fact that Mick doesn't want her to be autopsied and get around him on that. Not that they've not already taken blood and tissue samples from her and sent them off. This was done legally before he told anyone of her supposed wishes." Barkley got out of the car and put his hand in to help her out. Anyone of her brothers would have done the same thing, but it was different when a stranger did it. "I was just speaking to my family, and they're going to meet us all in town for some dinner. They'd gotten so wrapped up in what they were doing that they forgot they were having guests tonight."

"They don't have to do that." Barkley simply told her that it was his parents, and he didn't question them when they told him what to do. "Aren't you a little old to be afraid of your parents?"

"Old or not, I'm terrified of them." They all laughed and joked with Barkley about his fear. "I think I'm most afraid of disappointing them. Especially my mom. But the look on my dad's face when he feels like we didn't give something our best is something that I strive not to see again." She asked him what he'd done. "I pretended to be sick so that I'd not have to go school at the Sadie Hawkins dance. I hadn't gotten any of the girls to ask me."

"So it was your ego that got you into trouble." Barkley nodded while laughing. "I think that even knowing you as little as I do, your ego could take a few hits to it, and you'd come out on top. Besides, I doubt very much you have any trouble getting a date from anyone now. You're not too bad looking for a man."

"Thank you. I think." They entered the restaurant and were seated right away. They were in a large private room that was already made up and waiting for them. Christ, it was a fucking long table with what looked like a million chairs around it. "My brothers are coming as well. Jenson and Clay's wife, along with my grandma. You'll like her. She's a hoot. Well, I guess you'd like them all. They're all good people."

While they waited on the family, Barkley ordered some appetizers for them. When she took one of the stuffed mushrooms off the platter, she moaned at the taste. It was the best she'd ever eaten of the treat. When there were no more left, her having the most of them, she stabbed the one on Barkley's plate and stuck it into her mouth. She was both embarrassed as well as enjoying the look on his face when she looked at him.

"We should have warned you about Carrie. She loves food and will steal from strangers to have what she wants." Barkley nodded at Aaron, her other brother, then gave her the one that he'd hidden under the deep-fired ravioli that she didn't care for. "You should also protect your drinks. She's sneaky about taking the last sip of whatever we're all drinking.

When his family showed up, Carrie fell in love with them all. Especially Lisa, as she insisted they all call her. She also had pictures of the twins, also sharing how much she was enjoying them being around.

Chapter 3

Clay read over the contracts that he'd been sent twice. Then his father read them before Clay read them again. The NASA program was his to run. All he had to do was sign on the dotted line, so to speak. He looked up when Lizzy said his name.

"Shit, or get off the pot, Clay. You want the job, and all you need to do is sign it. Look. They even made it easy for you by putting little tabs where you need to put your name." He asked his wife why she was pushing him. "I'm not pushing you. Not really. I'm just tired of you looking that thing over like you're expecting something to leap out at you all of a sudden. Your dad even told you to sign it. You're getting the best deal he's ever seen. Not to mention all the perks that come my way when you're there."

Lizzy smiled at him. "You know I love you, right?" She told him that he'd better. "I do. Trust me. But I'm afraid to sign it, to be honest. I'm afraid that it will change us somehow."

"Change us into what?" He said he didn't want to be like the men he was replacing. "Not going to happen. I'll keep you on the straight and narrow when you start to look like that is your plan. Besides, since you're aware that it might happen, I have no doubt that you won't ever become them."

She sat on his lap and held him. All he could think about was just how much he loved his wife. And the fact that she loved him back was like ice cream with his favorite pie. She was the best that he'd ever seen.

"The house that they gave us when we needed to be in town for very long is nice. I love the fact that there are several bedrooms in it just in case your family wants to come and visit us while there." He said there would be plenty of room for their family as well. "Yes, there is that. While we're on the subject, I'm going to have your baby."

Clay was still sitting there when she got up and left him. He had to run it through his head several times before he could come to terms with what she'd said to him. Laughing and getting up, he sat back down long enough to sign where the tabs were. Putting it in the envelope that would send it via a courier, he went in search of his wife. His pregnant wife.

He found her in the kitchen with her dad. Since Clay didn't know who knew about the baby and she didn't mention it again, he listened in on the conversation that was going on between the two of them. Something about a job.

"I know that you can support me, honey, but I want to find me something to do. To get out and meet people again. I've only just realized how much time I'm spending by myself, and I don't like what thoughts enter my head. I need to become a member of society. Get out there and do something with my life." Alfred hugged his daughter as he continued. "You and Clay have given me a second chance at life. And I'm not going to waste it by feeling sorry for myself while waiting to die. I need to be productive to keep the demons away."

"Don't say things like that, Dad. I'm going to

have a baby soon, and I'm going to need you here to help out with it." Alfred pulled away from his daughter and asked her if she was serious. "Yes. Completely. But I've only told you and Clay, so let's not spread it around just yet."

He wasn't nearly as shocked by the news as he'd been. Picking Lizzy up, he swung her around and around until she begged him to let her go. When he hugged her again, Alfred reached for him to make it a group hug. Clay thought that it was one of the best hugs he'd had in all his life.

"I don't know what to do." Lizzy asked him if he still wanted to work because she had the perfect job for him. "All right. You tell me what it is, and I'll do it. I'm so happy right now that I could about bust. A baby in the family again. I don't know how much help I'll be with helping you, dear, but I'll start reading up on it right away. No. No, if I do that, check some books out of the library. Everyone in town will know about it before I make it home. No, we'll learn together, the three of us. My baby girl is having a baby."

Alfred continued to babble on about reading and books as he left them in the kitchen. His half-eaten sandwich was still on the counter, as was his glass of tea. He didn't bother moving it. Having been around Alfred for the past few months, he was sure he'd be back when he remembered that he'd made himself something. Pulling Lizzy into his arms, he held her tightly.

"I really don't want to tell anyone just yet. I'm still getting used to the idea myself. Having a baby in this family could be simply crazy. Your mom and grandma will be all over us, won't they?" He told her that they loved her. "And I love them. So much."

They spent the rest of the day going over things that they'd need for the new house. The government was picking up the tab on the house as well as furnishings, so Clay was all right with them shopping. Normally that was a thing that he most despised, shopping.

At four o'clock, they headed to his parent's home. Dad was going to show him the issues that he was having with his computer, not that he couldn't fix it himself. Clay thought that his dad was just making an excuse for them to have dinner together. They were just sitting down to dinner when his cell phone rang. Leaving the room to take the call when he saw who it was from, he stood outside on the back deck in the spring-like evening to speak to Alex Hardgrave.

"I've got your contracts, son. I'm so happy that you've agreed to come and work with us on this. Also, you should know that your back pay for the work that you've done for us so far is now in your account. Brock and I agreed that you should have been paid what a NASA employee should have been making instead of what they were paying you." He said that he'd enjoyed the work. "Yes, I'm sure that you did. And I'm so very happy that we've had you around despite the men that you were working for. My goodness, we're finding out things about those five men that I never would have thought of. Did you know that they would only put Jade on their outsourcing contract list rather than hiring her full-time? The things that she could have been doing for us. The two of you could have had all this taken care of by now. You know, the race to be the first of everything. Before I forget, however, it's not on your contract with us. Your family, from now until there are no more Strongs left of your lines, will enjoy free access to all the places here in DC. It's the least we can do for someone that done more for us in the last few months than had been done in the prior administration."

"I'm glad to do it. And I know that my family will enjoy the free trips to the museums and such. Lizzy and I are going to make a list of all of the sites and make sure to visit at least one of them each time we're there. Make a day of it." Alex said that sounded like an excellent idea. "Lizzy thought of it. She's forever keeping me in good graces with things." They both laughed. "We looked over some of the furniture ideas that you sent along for us. And put a few things into the cart as you suggested."

He looked at his dad when he came outside with him. He had a feeling that he'd been on the phone longer than he'd meant to and told Alex that he had to go and finish dinner with his family. Dad stopped him before he opened the door.

"We're moving out of this house for Jenson to move in. However, he doesn't want it. He said that he loves the home that he and Jade have and asked me to ask you if you and Lizzy would like it. It's a big house, and your mom and I are just too lonely here all by ourselves. It's entirely too big for just the two of us now." He asked his dad where they were going. "To your house if you'll allow it."

"It's big too." He said it was, but not as big as the Manor house was. "I'll have to talk to Lizzy. Like me, I think that she — well, all of us thought that Jenson and Jade would be moving into it."

"I did as well. I'm sort of glad that he's not, to be honest. It's a big house but not the kind that he needs being a congressman. He'll need a party room, and his home has that with the large ballroom on the upper floors." He'd forgotten about that part of Jenson's home. "So did I, to be honest. But he's got a good point. The family home is not big enough for fundraisers and the like. Not like he needs."

Going into the house, Dad brought up first about the Manor. He watched Lizzy's face as Dad explained the same reasons to her why Jenson wasn't going to be taking the family home. Then he offered it to them. Lizzy looked at him. She seemed as confused and excited as he was.

"What do you think, Clay? Would you like to move back into this house?" He told her that he would, actually, but so long as she was with him, he could live in a box and be happy. "You're being sappy again. Really. Would you like to live here? For the rest of our lives?"

"I would." Lizzy nodded and looked at his parents. "We'll do it. For no other reason than it would be a great home to raise the next generation of Strongs."

They didn't mention the baby, for which he was both sad and glad for. It would have been a large gathering when his entire family found out. They'd be there all night, too, speculating on the gender of the baby as well as anything else that they could and would dream up to talk about. His family was good at that. Talking.

While Mom showed Lizzy through the house, he and his dad sat in his office and talked about the things that were going on with the Cartwright family. The elder man, Michael, was a piece of work. And dad believed that he was responsible for a great many deaths that they'd not been able to attach to his name as yet.

"Do you know if there is a tool made that can see what's underground? I think there is, but for the life of me, I can't find a thing about it." Clay told his dad that there were ways of getting information like that from satellites. "So there wouldn't be any reason for Cartwright to know that we're looking into his property. I like that idea better. I've heard things about the man that frankly scares me. I know that his in-laws are around here. I wonder if he has any idea why they're here other than the death of their sister."

"Mick is stupid." He thought about it. "No, that's not right. He's not intelligent by any means but not stupid. When he was in your office the other day, I had a feeling that he was just as terrified as anyone that I've ever spoken to." Clay had a thought. "Could he be a victim of his father as well? And afraid of him?"

"You don't think that Mick is the one having sex with those babies then." It wasn't a question, but Clay thought that it did deserve an answer all the same and told him what he thought. "All right. Now that you feel the same way as I do about things, I'm going to tell you what I unearthed today when I was going through records. Mick was in and out of the hospital when he was a baby. Right up until he was about seven. I don't know that the abuse stopped then, but he was no longer getting looked at there. And back when he was a child, things like sexual abuse weren't talked about or even worried over as much as they are now. There is no way that he would have gotten by with that nowadays."

"So the mother knew as well. Do you think that Mattie knew what was going on?" Dad thought that she would have had to of known. "I guess you're right on that. With all the wounds on those little girls, she would surely have had to of noticed something was wrong."

He also thought about how the two women had been fighting over dresses for the girls. And the fact that Jane had had a gun on her when she'd gone shopping. He asked his dad if they knew if the gun was registered to anyone. Dad told him that it belonged to Michael but that Jane was also registered as a secondary user.

"She went there prepared to kill Mattie." Dad said that it looked like it to him. "Christ, Dad. Do you suppose that she was going to see someone about what was going on, and they got her out of the way? Or was it just getting her out of the—they wanted the girls full time. The grandparents. They didn't want to have to keep up appearances of getting a weekend with the girls and would have them all the time. Do you suppose that Mick knew about that, or were they planning to get rid of him as well?"

"I think that you're on the right track with what you're saying." Clay sat there in stunned silence while he thought of all the implications of what he knew about the family already. "I'm afraid that I'm in over my head with this one. Even with all the research we're doing and finding, I'm not sure that I could run a successful trial and win. Because to me, that is going to be the only outcome that will get the girls in a safe place."

For as much as he hated the idea that his father thought he was in over his head, he wasn't so sure that he wasn't correct. There was a great deal at stake with this thing they were gathering up information on. The lives of two little girls who had been abused enough, too, were counted in that information. Clay found himself being proud of his father right then. More so than he'd ever been before.

~*~

Barkley was enjoying being around the Boone family. They were all smart and had a great sense of humor. Even their sister, Carrie, was fun to be around. The best part was she gave as good as she got from her siblings, and Barkley thought that was the best part. Not that he teased her all that much. Being around her made him realize, too, that his sisters-in-law weren't so bad compared to her. Not that she was nasty mean, but she didn't ever hold back when she had something to say.

He'd never been around a woman with her family before. Neither of his sisters-in-law had a family that he could have interacted with. When he realized that families weren't like his, close and wealthy, he'd been trying his best to keep his body intact. All women, after he turned sixteen, decided that he was prime for the plucking, and they wanted to be plucked in the worse sort of way by him.

Barkley was a flirt. He knew that. It was legendary that he could get a date or two on the same night with both girls knowing about the other and not having a problem with it. Or so he'd thought.

He'd been seeing this girl in high school that seemed nice. Everyone seemed to like her. He soon found out that it was him they liked, and they were only tolerating her. Her personality was wonderful, and he had enjoyed hanging out with her. On occasion, she'd get too clingy or want more than he was willing to give, and they'd have a fight. Mostly it was about money and him not giving her any. But she would come back a few days later and tell him she was sorry. That got old quickly.

While on a date with another woman, he was knocked on the back of the head with something hard. They'd been at the movies and had had a good time. They were walking out to his truck when he'd been hurt. It hadn't knocked him out, not completely it did make him too dizzy to stand up for very long. When he was finally able to get around enough, he saw that the women were fighting each other. And viciously too.

After the police had been called, he was taken to the hospital first. No matter how many times they separated the two women, they'd be back at it again. After getting fifteen stitches in the back of his head, he found out that the women had fought with their nails and teeth. Even whatever they could find around them to use. The first woman had a broken arm and ankle as well as several hundred stitches on her body, mostly her face. While the jealous one had a broken ankle and a broken hand, as well as being shot by the police when she resisted arrest. To this day, he found himself looking around for the ridiculous woman. Just in case she was ever freed from prison. She'd been found guilty of attempted murder on his part, and the same for his date. He'd see the first woman once in a while around town. But all they did was say hi or nod and move on.

Barkley often wondered if the woman had blamed him for what had happened. He hoped not. Nothing he'd done would have encouraged the crazy woman that they were anything more than hanging out. He'd only been seventeen. Much too young to make any kind of long-term commitment, he'd told her. However, when taken to court, she told the judge that he'd raped her and she was going to have his child. After a ten-minute break to have her blood tested, she was taken to prison, and he was a much smarter kid when it came to picking dates.

Barkley needed to get some things from the shop in town. Dad wanted them to spend some time in the area, buy locally and to be friendly. He'd never had an issue with that, so he was happy that he needed to get out and get some things for his still coming together home. Carrie asked if she could hang out with him.

"I don't care. I love to walk, is that going to be all right with you?" She said she'd love that so long as he realized that her legs were shorter than his. "I think I can handle that. I was also going to pick up some lunch and take it back to my place. Would you like to join me?"

They were headed into the first shop when she told him what she wanted from the deli that had only recently opened up. After ordering what they were both going to have, he pulled a cart from the line and began pulling things off the shelf he'd come to get. Mostly it was staples of food, but he did need things like napkins and ice trays too.

"Don't you have one of those fancy refrigerators that spits out ice every ten seconds?" He said that he did, but with an ice tray, he could freeze some of his tea so that when it melted, he didn't have diluted tea. "That's a good idea. I might have to try that when I get home."

He finished up his grocery shopping and had the kid that worked there take them to his house. Barkley could have taken them himself in his car, but he was trying to help out the Morris family by giving Toby, their oldest son, some work to do.

"That was nice of you." Barkley explained to Carrie that he knew that the family was struggling and not working at the moment. This was the only way that he'd figured out how to get him the much-needed money. "Try a shopping card. I did that once for one of my workers. They were really struggling—they had a child with disabilities, and the government wasn't helping them at first. Anyway, I made it so that they won a gift card for being the hundredth in line that week or some bullshit. It worked out well for them because they could get all the groceries they needed for the week. Eating every day helped not just their child but themselves too."

"I'll have to do that sometime. However, they don't shop all that often. Lack of funds. I've even tried to find the two adults jobs, but it hasn't worked out for them." She said that he shouldn't be helping them then. Not if they were not willing to work. "That's what my mom and dad said. And the reason that I give the money to Toby. He uses it for school supplies as well as fees that he has. If he does well in school, which he is on the honor roll each term, I'll help him get to college."

"You are a nice guy, aren't you? And not nearly as dumb as I thought you were." They teased and kidded around as they made their way to the next shop. Barkley stopped suddenly and turned to Carrie, holding her still. "What is it?"

"I know that you can take care of yourself. I'm also aware that you can do whatever you want and that I would support you. But right now, I want you to stay behind me and keep your mouth closed. I'm not being macho or mean, but please? Do as I ask." She nodded and looked around him just enough that he knew that she could see the two people coming toward them. "That is your brother-in-law and his dad. I don't want them to know that you're in town. For any reason. All right?"

"Yes. All right." When he turned toward the two men, he felt Carrie put her hands at his sides. Feeling better, knowing that she'd stay put, he spoke to the two men. They'd know him because he'd been at the mall when the women had been shot.

"Mr. Strong. I've been looking for you." He

asked him what he wanted. "How about you get rid of that woman there, and we can talk man to man." Her fingers dug deeply into his sides, but he didn't so much as wince at the pain. "You and I need to get things straight about how my wife supposedly killed off Mattie. Now, I believe you got things all turned around. I want you to remember that you saw a gun in Mattie's hands too. That my wife, my dear wife, was defending herself."

"But that's not what I saw. Your wife pulled out a gun and shot Mattie. They both fell down, but it was Mattie that wasn't able to get back up. They were fighting over dresses for your granddaughters." Michael told him that part was fine to remember, but the rest of it was just wrong. "No. Even the videos that were taken by the police show that your wife pulled a gun first. And shot Mattie while she was arguing with her with her over the sale of them."

"Like I said, you can remember that part if you want, but you're going to remember too that there was a second gun." Barkley asked him where that gun was supposed to have come from and where was it now. "You just remember like I tell you to, and I'll take care of the rest. I'm a man that gets shit done, and you're going to be doing that for me. I might even be able to slip you some money, too, if you do a good job."

"I don't need nor want your money." Michael laughed. "Did you know that your granddaughters had been beaten the morning that the shooting had gone on? That when the doctor on site examined them, they were in a bad way? They're just infants. Why would anyone do that to them?"

"None of your business, young man. Not one bit of what happens with my family is shit to you. Do you hear me? Now. We're going to go over what you remembered once more, then I'm going to go to the police station with you. You know, just in case you forget something. You want to get this right the first time, Strong. If you don't, there is no telling what might happen to you. I don't want to be bogged down with a trial when I'm going to have to help my son here raise them girls to be good citizens around here." Barkley asked if he was threatening him. "No. Goodness no. That's against the law. I was just trying to help you out so that you don't end up on a slab like my wife and favorite daughter-in-law did. I bet your family wouldn't like that any more than I did."

"Did you plan out the killing of Mattie, Michael?" The flash of pure rage came over his face nearly too quickly for him to see. But it was there, and Barkley had seen it. "You'd better be careful, Michael. Someone might be upset if you go around telling people what they should be remembering as opposed to what they actually saw. I know that I saw, and that's what I'm going to keep telling the police when asked. And when this goes to trial, I see no reason to believe that it won't—two people were murdered, then I'll keep saying the same thing. That your wife and only your wife had a gun and that she shot the other woman. Then when your wife wouldn't put her gun down, the police killed her when she fired at an officer."

"That's not going to be told either, young man. I'm working on that now." Mick whispered to his father. "My wife was shot by Mattie because she had a gun. You remember that, right? Then my wife, in defending herself, shot back."

"Really? That's the story that you're going to stick with? Then how do you suppose your wife ended up with thirty-one bullet holes in her body? Mattie—

who didn't have a gun at all would have had to have over five revolvers in order to have pulled that off. And the police didn't even find one? How the hell do you think that is going to go over when you bring that up?" He told him he was a big man around here. "So I've heard. Wasn't it you that broke the lawn chairs that the ice cream place puts out for paying customers? Not that you have ever paid for much in your life, but I heard that about you." Michael lunged at him, and he felt Carrie pull him back.

"Listen here, you little fucker. You'll do what you're told, or I'm going to pop you so full of holes that your momma won't even know who you are. You're going to do what I said, you hear me?" Barkley said that he heard him as Carrie was pushing him into the shop next to where they were standing. "You'd better do the right thing, Strong, or so help me, you'll regret it."

Barkley was breathing hard when Carrie turned him around and slapped him across the face. Just as he was going to ask her what the hell that was for, she hit him again. This time with her fist doubled up and all her anger directed at him.

When he fell back, trying his best to grab onto anything that would keep him from hitting his head, he felt the floor hit him there twice before he just succumbed to the blinding pain that he was suddenly in. The last thing he heard when he was going out was Carrie calling him a fucking moron. He thought that his family would agree with her.

Chapter 4

Carrie was so angry that she could have easily taken out a contract on the man lying on the hospital gurney next to her. The idiot had actually got into an argument with a man who they all knew was a murderer. Not only that, but when threatened by him, the lummox had kept telling him that he wasn't going to cooperate with him. Lie. That's all he had to do was to fucking lie to him and say, 'Why yes, I'll remember it your way.' But no, he had to—

"You're grumbling again." She glared at Barton. "You're wasting your time in glaring at me. Have you met my mom? I mean, even my grandma is better at glaring than you are."

"Are all you Strong men stupid?" Barton nodded and told her that they were. Especially when protecting a woman. "Just like that? You're going to agree with me? What is wrong with you guys? He threatened him? Not just with that, either. He actually told him that he was going to kill him off. What the fuck? Does Barkley have a death wish? And he wasn't protecting me. He was keeping me out of harm's way."

"How is that not protecting?" This time she stood up. "You're very cute when you're trying to be all huffy. I'm sure that you have a meaner streak in you, but right now, since I know that you're both just fine, I think you're adorable."

"No woman who is pissed off wants to be called cute or adorable. Damn it all to fuck and back. You're all certifiable." She stared pacing the little cubby they were in. The hospital was going out of its way to make sure that Barkley was all right. She and Barton too, but she was too pissed off to be thankful that he wasn't hurt more. "I know that I shouldn't have hit him, but he wasn't taking Cartwright seriously."

"Yes, I was." Barkley started to sit up on the gurney he was on, but she pushed him back down.

"You're very bossy, aren't you? And as for what I was doing, you might well have missed that we were standing right next to a camera in the store we went in. That—you hit me."

"I shouldn't have hit you twice. Once was enough. But I was so—what does that camera have to do with the way you were acting?" He told her. That deflated her anger a bit. "I didn't know that it had sound too. You egged him on so that he'd confess to something. What exactly did he confess to? Nothing. That's what."

"Yes, he did. He threatened me. Not only with bodily harm, but he offered me money too if I were to change my story to the one that he wanted me to say." She said that he'd bribed him. "Bingo. It's all recorded too. Not only will Michael be arrested, but since his son spoke to him at one point, feeding him information, I've no doubt, then he'll be arrested as well. I don't know about you, but knowing that he's not out roaming around to do what he wants makes me feel a good deal better."

"Now that you put it like that, I do as well." Carrie glared at him again. "You could have been killed."

"It would have been on the recording too." It hurt her that he was so cavalier about his own life, it seemed to her. She turned on her heel and left him there. Carrie could hear him calling for her as she left the room and headed to the exit out of the emergency department.

It didn't take her long to get to the road. Still upset with Barkley, she cursed him and called the man every name that she could think of under her breath. When Barton caught up with her, she told him to go away. That she needed time to not just cool off but to burn off some energy as well.

"He's upset. Not at you but that he's upset you." She told him good, then pleaded with Barton to go back to his brother. "I was told to stay with you, and that's what I'm going to do. He doesn't want you to meet up with the Cartwrights. They've not been arrested as yet that we know of, and even if he didn't know who you were, he'd have seen that you were with Barkley and used you against him. If I were evil, that's what I'd do. Please. I need to stay with you."

She stopped in her tracks and turned to look at Barton. Stress and anger made her cry, and she was doing so now. When he told her not to cry that Barkley would murder him, she asked him why he'd do something so stupid as that.

"He likes you, I guess. We all do." Carrie said that she liked him and all the Strongs as well. "I agree with him on you being out alone. As I said, even if Michael got a glimpse of you while the two of you were together, he might retaliate by coming after you. I'm not saying that is going to happen, but in my experience, stupid people don't think beyond what they want to happen."

"Cartwright threatened your brother." Barton nodded and said that the police had arrived when he'd come to get her. "I'm sorry that he sent you out. I'm sure you would rather be with him than out chasing some woman."

"Nah. I love chasing women." She giggled when he smiled at her. "Good, you can still see the humor in things. But Barkley was right in making him pissed off enough to have him threaten him. They'll arrest them simply because of who we are."

"The great Strongs. Are you all as wealthy as I've heard you are?" He shook his head and told her they were more than likely more wealthy. She stared at him. "You're not kidding, are you? You've more than a few million dollars at your disposal, do you?"

"More like a few billion at our disposal." He put out his arm so that she'd take it. But she was too busy thinking about what he'd said. "First of all, my dear friend, I'm happy that you didn't believe that we were as wealthy as we are. It means that we're not showing off what we have. My parents and their several generations back parents were smart businessmen and women." She put her arm through his, and they made their way back to the hospital. "As a family, we're extremely wealthy. But even as individuals, we're still extremely moneyed too. I think that Jenson has the most with several billion in investments and money, thanks in part to him marrying Jade, who was wealthy before meeting him. Then Barkley. He's always been the smartest with money. That's the reason that he's in charge of the real estate part of our wealth. He also does investments for us all that keep us able to use our money for things that we want."

He continued telling her about each of his brothers and parents. Explaining to her that they had put wings on the hospital when it had been needed.

Purchased items for other countries that had one thing happen or the other. Barton also told her that they each worked too when they could.

"Not work so much as volunteered. If we do get paid, the money is invested in whatever project that is near and dear to us at the time, and it works out for everyone." Carrie asked about Jenson running for Congress. "Yes, he'll get there, we hope. Since he's been married to Jade, he's had talks with our family about running for president in a few years. I can see the two of them being there for a bit."

"You talk to each other about everything then." Barton told her that they did. Simply because they want to make sure that we're all on the same line of things so we have backup. "And if one of you disagrees about what one wants? What happens then?"

"Most of the time, we will do it anyway if it's only one person. But we do listen to why they have their opinion. But if it's more than that, the project or idea is set aside until things are thought through more. Usually, not always, but usually things work out the way they should be." The police were in the cubby with Barkley, and when he saw her, he asked her if she was all right. Nodding at him, he looked so relieved that she felt her heart flutter. She wondered if her brothers would be that relieved if she'd been pissed off enough to hit one of them and then stalk off the way that she had. Probably not.

"We picked up the recordings that you mentioned. They've been gone over, and I have some of my best men, along with some agents that are in town, to go and pick the two of them up. They're living in a house that we didn't have a record of when we made it so that they'd not be able to get any money from their estates. That will be the best way of keeping them in town while we do research. As it stands right now, we're taking a deeper look into what else we might have missed." Barkley asked about the satellite that was being used for the property. "We've been lucky there so far too. While our local police station is not involved in that part of it, we have been asked to help with digging and such if there is a need. And from what I've heard and read in the morning reports, there will be some digging."

Carrie didn't know what that meant, but she was sure that someone would tell her if she asked. And she would. After the police were gone. Taking both hers and Barkley's statements as to the threats that had been thrown at them, the police asked if they wanted to have a guard on his curtain while he was there.

"No. I'm going to be released soon, I hope. I know that I have a slight concussion, but if I behave myself at home, then I can stay there." Carrie couldn't help it. She snorted at the idea that he could behave himself. "I will. You'll see. Besides, I think your brother Neal went to the airport to pick up the wives. This might take a bit longer than we had first thought. I don't know about you guys, but I'm excited to meet the rest of your family."

"Are you sure about this? I mean, they all have children. Robert and Dan don't, of course, but they could get a call at any time to adopt. But Neal and his wife Paula, they have four and one on the way." It was Barton that assured her that they'd be fine. "All right. But don't say that you weren't warned. They can be a lot when they're all together like this."

When she got a call from her brother Robert, asking her to explain to the family that he didn't have a wife like the others, she told him that she'd do that.

Where to start on something like that wasn't anything that she was sure about. So as soon as she got off the phone, she told both Barkley and Barton that her brother was a homosexual.

"Okay? Did you think that we'd care?" Carrie told them that she wasn't sure about people and her brother's sexuality. "I can understand that. But really, it makes no difference to us. Nor do I think they'll have any trouble with anyone in town. I'm not saying that everyone will be accepting, but for the most part, no one will care."

"I hope not. I don't want my brothers hurt." Barton told her that he'd take care of anyone that said anything. "Robert and Dan can handle themselves. They've gotten used to hiding out in plain sight. But, as I said, I don't want either of them hurt."

"I'm sorry that they have gotten used to that. I can understand, too, that it's not something that everyone can get behind. But I swear to you that he'll be protected along with Robert. Frankly, it's none of our business what the two of them do or, for that matter, who someone loves." She thanked Barkley. "You're welcome. And I was serious. If anyone gets out of hand, then you tell one of us, and we'll make sure that your brothers don't have anyone hurting them. That's a promise that I can keep for you and them."

She didn't know what to think about that. People say things like that, being accepting of people when they're only mouthing the words and not saying them to be honest. Carrie decided that she was going to wait and see what happened. Looking at the two brothers as they talked about Cartwright, she had a feeling that they were sincere about what they said and would actually make sure that everyone was all right.

~*~

Barkley was glad to be home. He was getting around all right. Having a headache wasn't nearly as bad as he knew that it could have been, but he was home and not dead. Thinking about what Cartwright had told the police made him a little ill. The man did indeed have an evil streak in him. About as wide as the man was tall, Barkley thought.

Heading to the kitchen, he wasn't surprised to find Carrie there with Dan and Robert. Dan was going through the cabinets, looking for supplies, he told Barkley since he was going to be cooking dinner tonight. Everyone was going to meet at his home so that they could have a nice meal and see the babies. They were going to be coming here tonight so that the wives could get a look at them. Whatever that meant to women, he thought with a laugh.

Since all of Carrie's brothers had children, with the exception of Robert, Mom thought it would be a good idea if they each took a family apiece into their homes. That way, the children would have more room than they would at a hotel to run around and be kids. Also, since their homes were so close together, they could still see one another and talk.

"You had enough yet?" He asked Carrie what she meant. "Last night, I thought for sure you were going to run them off, but you didn't. Today, you don't look like you've slept a wink. Are you all right?"

"Yes. A terrible headache, of course, but I enjoyed the kids. I'm glad now that Dad and Mom put up the swing set this year, and the pool has been a huge hit for them." She said that she'd been enjoying it as well. "I'm glad. I think that Jenson was afraid it would be too cold to use his. Which is fine. The one there has been ready to go since winter. I love a refreshing swim year-round. How about you?"

"I will take it when I can get it." The two of them sat at the bar in the kitchen, and Robert handed him a large glass of ice water and two pain pills. "I'm going to just take one of them right now. I'm better at handling the pain, and I don't want to be drowsy when the family comes over."

"You take two of them. That way, when they get here later, you'll be coming out of the medication and feeling better. But if you still have a headache when they get here, then you can take one." He took the two pills when Robert stared at him. With a smile, he continued about what the plan was for the day. "Dan and I are going to go into town with your truck. Are you still sure that's all right with you?"

"I am fine with that. I told you. I have my car in the garage if I need to go anywhere." His cell phone rang, and he pulled it out of his pocket. "Christ, it's business. Carrie, are you going to hang around here with me? This call might take a while."

"Why don't I go with them? I have a few things that I didn't pack with me to come here. You can take care of business, and I can as well." He asked her if she was sure. "I'm very sure. When I come back, if it's the ass you were telling me about, then you can tell me how much you actually paid for the building that he didn't pay shit for."

He didn't know what possessed him, but he kissed her on the forehead as he left the kitchen. Heading back to his office to take the call, he was pulling up the email he'd gotten from the guy as he was going on about the offer on his property.

"I've been looking into your property that you said you inherited, Mr. Chase. According to the records that I was able to pull up, you don't actually own that land. You never have. Your mother left it to your sister. Nothing at all to you. I believe you were told that when you went to the hearing of the will. Was that what happened?" Mr. Chase had wanted four million for his land simply because a Strong had wanted to purchase it. "Why should you think that I'm going to pay you for something that you don't even own? And I've have to be pretty stupid to pay you anything for land that I'm well aware of that you don't own. Your sister was fairly pissed off when I told her that you were trying to sell it out from under her."

"She's a fool and will sell whatever she has worthy to the first person that shows her a shiny coin. Women should never have access to money. They'll go through it faster than a kid with a chocolate bar. You'll be dealing with me with this land. I'm a good deal smarter than she is, and I know how to make a buck off of nothing. This land, this is mine to do with as I want. That way, I can get enough for my sister and I to share. Minus my percentage for selling it, of course." Barkley told Chase that he was having better luck talking to Rebecca. "I'm telling you right now, Strong. If you screw me out of this deal, I'm going to sue you. Becky doesn't have a head for money. She'll piss it all away, and I'll be left holding the bag when there's nothing left. No. You'll deal with me on this, or so help me, I'll take you to court."

"Good luck with that. And you might want to look into what your sister has been doing for the last ten years or so. She's a very smart businesswoman." Chase snorted. "Also, it might come as a surprise to you to know that she's been paying the taxes on the house as well as keeping your mom in medications since you ran off with her fortune ten years ago. I don't believe, according to your mom's attorney, she liked you all that much. Even before you decided to become the asshole that you are. You didn't even come to visit her when she requested to see her only living son."

"What does she need to see me for? I'm the same man that was there when I was living there. I didn't steal her money either. I knew that she'd get that all wrong in the end. Mom *lent* it to me, and I never got around to paying her back before she died, that's all. Now it's all water under the bridge. She's dead, and I'm going to get my fair share of money since Mom didn't have the sense to leave me anything in her will. It's mine. All of it should be mine since I'm the oldest living male in her family." Barkley asked what happened to his brothers. "Weaklings. All of them. They got a cold, and the next thing that happened to them they were pushing up daisies. Even our father didn't have the sense to come in out of the cold, and he died because of it."

"Becky is in charge now. Do you want to know what that means or should mean to you?" Chase asked him why he'd say something like that to him when he'd just told him he was going to take over the sale of the land. "She's asked me to tell you that she's having your parents exhumed as well. Also, your younger brothers. It was the last thing that her mother told her to do before she died. Poor woman. She suffered badly towards the end of her life. Mostly from what I understand, thanks to you. Who steals their mother's pain pills when she's at the end stages of their life? But I guess you wouldn't know since you refused to go and see your own mother. Could she know something that the rest of the world doesn't? Becky seemed in a hurry to get someone to sign off on the exhumation paperwork to get them tested."

"What the hell is she thinking? Damn it all to hell. See? Right here? That's what I'm talking about. She's forever sticking her nose into things that don't concern her." Carrie came out and handed him a note. He'd gotten a phone call, and she'd taken a message for him. He read it as Chase went on and on about how his sister needed to keep her trap closed. "Damn it all the fuck and back. I'm going to hire you. You're my attorney, and you're going to sue her into keeping her mouth shut before I have to shut it for her."

"I'm not going to be able to do that, Mr. Chase. Your sister has hired my father as her attorney, and that would be a conflict of interest for us all." He asked him why. "Because, frankly, none of us like you. You're a bastard that took advantage of an elderly woman, your mother no less, and that doesn't set well with any of us."

"You would have done the same thing given the chance, and you know it." He said that his mother would have knocked the crap out of him, and then so would his father and brothers. "There you go right there. You don't know how to handle yourself. Knock them around a bit, and they'll see reason. If not, then you just give them a bit of juice that will take them out of the equation. Then when they get lippy, you give them a bit more until they're no problem." Barkley didn't know what to say to the man. Carrie took his phone from him and put it on speaker just as Chase was laughing. Dad joined them on the steps with his phone recording everything that was being said. "That there is the reason that you need to keep my sister from doing what she is doing. I don't need anyone digging up bodies right and left that—hell, digging up any one of them would get me in deep shit. And that isn't anything that I want. You shouldn't either if you know what's good for you."

"So, what you're telling me is that you knocked around your own family, and when that didn't get you what you wanted, you resorted to poisoning them? Christ man, is there nothing you won't do for a few bucks." He said that the estate was worth millions. "No, that's where you're wrong. The estate, as you call it, only consists of the land, which is in your sister's name. Which begs the question, why didn't you kill her off when you were shortening the lifetime of your other family members?"

"She wasn't worth the spit that made her. She's a woman. Christ, man. Haven't you been listening to a word I've been saying to you?" Barkley told him that he was listening to every word he said. "Then you understand that I never thought that she'd be worthy of my attention. Come to find out, she's the one that I should have been watching. And now I can't find the bitch. I don't suppose you know where she is, do you?"

"Even if I did, I'd not tell you. You'd just try and kill her off." The man laughed and said that he should have years ago. "You're nothing but a piece of shit, aren't you? You'd kill off your family instead of getting a job. Or, for that matter, being kind to your mother and family. Instead, you killed them all off one at a time in order to get what you wanted all along. When that took too long, you restored to killing them. Now you're sitting on your ass, wondering why you're not a part of the family. What little is left, anyway." He looked at his dad, who was holding up a piece of paper that he'd written on. "The bodies have been exhumed as of an hour ago. They're being taken care of right now. It's a shame, really, that you went to such great links to get what you wanted, and now you're going to prison."

Closing the connection, he stood up. He needed to take a walk. Or a run. Setting off toward the road, he decided that he was going to have to walk for miles with how he was feeling. When Carrie started to follow him, he turned to her, ready to tell her to go away, when he realized she was crying. All his pent-up anger disappeared when she sobbed and wrapped her arms around him. Holding her in his arms, he let her cry. When she looked up at him after a few minutes, he asked her what was wrong.

"He killed his entire family for money." He

nodded and told her that there were a lot of bastards out there. "I know, but I'd give anything to have a few more minutes with my parents. Even my sister, though, I'd not spoken to her in decades. Just ten minutes to tell her that even though I'd not known her all that well, I still loved her."

They walked for about a mile before either of them spoke. He liked hanging out with Carrie and her brothers. They were nothing like his brothers in that they seemed to enjoy arguing about little things. Also, they weren't as close as he was to his brothers. Not that he liked them better, but they were just different. Something that he'd grown to realize was that his family was nothing like others. Laughing a little, he told Carrie what he'd been thinking about.

"I can see that. I've thought the same thing about your brothers and you. You guys aren't perfect, but you have each other's back. Even when you guys think that the conversation that you're all having is getting loud, you check yourself and start over. Mine just keeps getting louder and louder. Then instead of figuring out a solution or whatever, they just walk away. Not you guys. You work well together. And I have to admit,

I'm so jealous of your parents. They're funny without being stuffy like you'd think rich people would be." He told her thanks. "You're welcome. What are you going to do about John Chase? I'm assuming that you have some sort of plan."

"I don't. I mean, I have a plan to knock the crap out of him if I see him, but other than that, my dad is working on the case." She asked him if he was also working on hers. "Yes. He's got about enough evidence to take it to a pretrial hearing. With your in-laws in jail, it's only a matter now of bringing them in. They're bitching about how they've been wrongly accused. I suppose that's what I'd say, too, if I knew I was going to go to prison for the rest of my life. Especially Michael. Dad has been getting reports of a disturbance in the ground surrounding the house that he lives in. While that doesn't one hundred percent mean a body, they're all confident enough to go there in a couple of days and start digging. That'll be easier with them both in jail too."

"Yes, I'm thinking that he'd be out there with a gun blowing people away for digging up the dead." She shivered. "The links that people will go to in order to get what they want. I'm thinking that I'm glad that I didn't know my sister's family. There is no telling how long we might have been alive had they known about us."

"Yes. I can see your brothers and you getting into their shit about how they were raising those babies." He stopped walking. "Look, my brother lives right there. Would you like to go and see them? They're doing really well now."

"I was warned not to go and look at them, or I'd be taking them home with me." She looked at his brother's home. "Just don't let me hold them. I can't know if my maternal instincts will kick in with just a look, but holding them will just put me in place of their mother."

He was still laughing as they approached Clay's home. He'd been holding them every chance he'd get. They were so calming to him. Even when they were upset and crying, he could get such a burst of energy from trying to get them to quiet down that he found himself at his brother's house daily just for the boost.

Of course, he never told anyone that. He would be made fun of for days, if not years. No, he kept things that he knew would make him a target to himself. It was better on his ego if he didn't.

As soon as Clay opened the door, he shoved a crying baby into Carrie's arms. Then when Lizzy came to the door with the other one sobbing too, she did the same thing. Carrie looked bewildered as she held the twins in her arms. When he reached for one, thinking to help her out, she told him to back off. Laughing as he led her to the living room, she held her nieces for an hour before allowing anyone else to hold them. As it turned out, they liked their aunt as much as she seemed to be liking them. Who knew?

Chapter 5

Robert found his sister in the office. She'd been missing, he supposed, for the last couple of hours. Barkley had left for work, and he said he'd be home late. While gone, they expected their sister to come into the living room with them as they went over contracts for Barkley that were for the new property that he had purchased.

"Carrie?" She didn't so much as move. Going further into the room, he touched his fingers to her shoulder, and she turned and looked at him. There were stains of tears on her face, and it bothered him that maybe Barkley had said something to her. "What happened? Did he say something to you?"

"Who?" Robert told her who he was talking

about. "No. He'd not do that to me. I think he likes me. I love him."

He'd known that Robert thought. That his sister was in love with Barkley. It was difficult to tell what he felt for her as the man was nearly as hard to read as Dan was. Sitting in the chair that was across from the big desk, he tried to think how to tell his little sister that he'd seen her love for Barkley just yesterday.

"He's a good man." He agreed with her. "He's been nothing but kind to all of us. Even when he's upset, which isn't all that often, he still goes out of his way to be nice to everyone. And he loves his parents. I like them too."

"Have you told Barkley that you love him yet?" She shook her head and looked out the window behind her. "Carrie, what's holding you back? You love him. You should tell him and soon."

"I'm not going to do that." Asking her why the hell not, she smiled at him. "Because he has it all. Money. Prestige. He even has you guys wrapped up and friendly with him. I'm just me. Carrie Boone that barely has a high school education. I work at a job that I loathe. But it pays the bills. I don't even have anything about me that makes me stand out from other dark-haired women. No tantalizing eye color. Blue isn't all that uncommon. I'm thin, no boobs to speak of, and I'm too tall for most men."

"But all those things are special to us." She tisked at him. Robert laughed. "You're beautiful, Carrie. You look so much like Mom that sometimes I find myself thinking you're her. Mattie looked like Dad. In all the wrong ways. However, if you don't let Barkley know that you love him, I will."

"No, you won't." He wouldn't, at least, he didn't think that he would. Robert wasn't sure how she knew that. "I'm ready to go back home too. I need to before Bethany and Sunny take more of my heart. Did I tell you that I spent the evening with them last night? They are adjusting so well after what's happened to them."

"They would. They're just babies, and I don't know that they'll remember what has happened to them. At least, I hope not. Why are you leaving? You're not staying for the trial? To make sure that they get what they deserve?" She said that she was going to talk to Mick. "Why? I mean, he'll just tell you more lies and expect you to believe him. I don't want you to go home, Carrie. What if they're not as accepting of me and Dan after you leave?"

"You don't believe that any more than I do." He said he was grasping at straws to keep her around. "You're going to have to try harder. That one is just stupid. You and Dan have made more friends in the last few weeks here than I think you did all during high school."

"You're right. Have you always been so stubborn?" She just stared at him. "I guess you have. But honey, I don't want you to miss out on something wonderful like being in love with a great person. And I don't think there are any better than Barkley. Any of them, really, but Barkley is the best."

"Barkley is the best at what?" There he stood in the doorway, looking at them both with a sandwich halfway to his mouth. "You all should stay here forever. Of course, I'd have to join a gym or something. Because the way that Dan cooks would be a killer for me to eat—"

"Carrie is in love with you." He looked at his sister and stuck out his tongue. "I told you I was going to tell him. And now I'm going to go to the kitchen and tell Dan that we have to find us a home close to you guys. I want to be an uncle in the worse kind of way." Robert stood up and closed Barkley's mouth. "Go to her, you nutball, before she changes her mind."

He was nearly to the kitchen when he turned around, going back to the still standing man and shoved Barkley into the office. He couldn't do everything for the man, but he did close the door. Smiling, he headed to the kitchen to tell Dan what had just happened. The two of them had been speculating for days about the couple, and he was glad that he'd gotten the opportunity to let Barkley know that someone loved him as much as he did Dan. Dan was jealous that he'd not been able to tell Barkley that Carrie loved him.

"What do you say that we go and put in a bid on that house on Fifth Street. It's the perfect home for the two of us." Robert sat at the counter as Dan continued. "We'll make a fortune off the house back home the way that we've renovated it."

"What about our stuff? I mean, we've been collecting things for that house since we met. Are you willing to just let it go too? I am if that helps you with your answer." Dan told him that he'd just as soon not ever have to go back there again, not after the send-off they were given when they came here. "I know. I had no idea that our neighbors were so…I guess we should have figured it out sooner, but to be honest with you, Dan, I think I didn't want to know that they thought of us as terrible people."

"No, neither did I." Dan poured him a glass of tea and sat down on the stool next to where he was. "Not once since we've been here have we had one person treat us any differently than they do the Strongs. I'm not so naïve to think that it's our personalities that have had them welcome us so much as it was the Strongs. But the townspeople have been really accepting of us even when we're not with them. Mrs. Daniels even came over yesterday to ask me to help her out with the dinner party she was having."

"She even invited us to go." They'd had a great time too. Not once did they feel like they'd been invited over because she wanted to show off the gays that lived in town. "Mr. Burgess' party that he threw was hurtful. The fact that he wanted us to wear a sign that said that we were faggots turned my stomach. The fucking bastard."

They'd been invited to the dinner party back home that was for the street party and how it was going to be handled this year. He and Dan had always donated money to the street-wide cookout and get-togethers. But they'd never gone. When they were at the door, Mr. Burgess' wife told them that they had to wait a minute. She had something to give them. Then her husband gives them both a sign that said 'I'm with the faggot' to wear so no one would forget. Dan had wanted to stay and embarrass the older man, but he'd wanted to just go home.

It wasn't that he was ashamed of what he was. He loved Dan and would tell anyone that. But to be made the ass of a party with signs no less was too much. The two of them vowed to never have anything to do with the people on their street again. Then this thing with Mattie had happened.

"Do you think that your sister, Mattie, would have felt the same way about us as the Burgess and the rest of the street had?" Robert told Dan that he hadn't any idea what she would have done. He didn't know her at all. "That's what Carrie said when I asked her. That she more than likely would have been cruel to us but that she wasn't sure anymore."

"Let's not go down that street, Dan. All right?" He nodded, and Robert was glad. "We'll make an offer on the house, and we'll sell everything that we left behind. We'll find us an attorney or, better yet, have Barkley find someone to take care of it all for us. Then once it's finalized, we'll just pretend that nothing ever happened to us and that we're here where we should have been all along. What do you think?"

"Perfect." They both turned to the door down the hallway. Dan smiled at him. "You think that we're going to be related to the Strongs soon? I can't think of a better person than Barkley to love Carrie. They both seem so suited to each other."

"It worries me a little, to be honest, that the two of them seemed to not understand that they've been in love for the last week or so. I think they started out as friends and are still, but Carrie caught on first that she was in love with the man. Hopefully, we're right, and Barkley is in love with her as well." Dan asked him if he thought they were wrong about Barkley loving Carrie. "I don't think so, but we could be. I don't want it to be only something that we *want* to see happen between the two of them. I'd hate that she is in love with him, and he only sees her as a buddy. Someone to hang out with and such. They do that a great deal. Hang out, I mean. Just yesterday, I heard them arguing. It was about how his mood was affecting her. Then they laughed. They're either in love with each other, or they need help. They're mentally off otherwise."

They were both laughing when Dan's phone went off. He used it to time things, and when he got up to take something out of the oven, Robert felt his mouth water. His cookies were the best he'd ever eaten. But his homemade bread would make him want to do just about anything for the first slice. Often times Dan would bake a loaf of bread, and they'd eat the entire thing for dinner. Just that and a salad, of course, to balance things out. With them being guests in someone else's home, he figured he'd have to share with Carrie and Barkley.

"He'd better understand how much I like him if I'm willing to share hot homemade bread with him." Dan agreed as he sliced up thick slices of the still-steaming treat. "Bring on the butter, Dan, so that I can pretend that there aren't about seven thousand calories in this one slice."

"I made another loaf for dinner tonight. We'll eat this one quickly, then I'll pull out the second one to bake." They were both laughing as they tried to cram half a slice of the too-hot bread in their mouths while talking about dinner. Christ, he loved Dan and thought everyone should be as happy as they were. "Oh, Ms. Lisa sent over some strawberry jam for us. I'll get it now."

He didn't care if he weighed eight hundred pounds. Robert was going to enjoy his lunch of bread and jam if it was the last thing he did today. It smelled like fresh strawberry pie to him. He was so happy they were moving here soon.

~*~

Barkley stared at Carrie when they were shut up in his office. She was avoiding looking at him for some reason, and he wanted her full attention. When she started talking about going to see Mick, he raised his hand up. He wanted her to stop talking about anything but what Robert had told him before leaving.

"You love me." He wasn't sure if he asked her or told her, but she said that she did. With all her heart.

"Why didn't you tell me? I mean, we've been together a lot the last several days. Or am I asking the wrong question? When did you realize that you loved me?"

"Yesterday, when we were taking a walk into town. You were telling me about the people that were out in front of their shops. You also mentioned their families and how you needed to get a few gifts for the butcher's daughter's wedding. Most rich people could care less what the butcher is doing, much less his daughter getting married. But there you were, telling him how much you were looking forward to going to it and that you couldn't believe that Tess was old enough to be getting married. Isn't she about your age?" He said that she was two years older. "I see. Then how is it that you're disbelieving of her being old enough to marry?"

"I was teasing her dad. He's a good man. It's her second marriage. I don't know if you knew that or not. Her first husband, Levi, I think his name was, went out one night to check on the cows and never returned. They'd been married about three months by then." She asked him what had happened to the man. "He messaged her about a week later. After all of us had been searching everywhere for him. Levi told her that he didn't want to live in a small town and that he had better things to do with his life rather than to be married to the butcher's daughter. I don't know what made him change his mind about Tess and her family. Doug has been a butcher for all his life. His dad before him and him before the son. Four generations of butchers. What Levi failed to understand or know was that Tess was wealthy. So was her father. When Tess was eighteen, she purchased a lottery ticket for the big lotto that goes on once a week. She was the only winning number. My dad helped her set up the winnings so that they could live off of it. Tess had never told Levi that—why do you love me?"

"Oh, that's easy. You're kind. Funny. You do what you say you will. That's a biggie to me. I don't like it when someone says they'll do something and don't. But you always do. But also, if you find a place where you're not going to be able to do what you said, you tell the person and find someone else that will do it. You're wonderful to your parents and are, I think, slightly afraid of them." He told her that he was. A great deal. "However, you respect them. Always."

"I guess those are good reasons to love me, but that's not really why, is it? I mean, what do I do that has made you fall in love with me?" She smiled, and Barkley felt his heart do a triple beat. "I've never thought of being in love with you. That didn't come out right. What I mean is, I thought of you as a good friend, the best I've had. But when you said that you loved me, or Robert did, my heart seemed to wake up then and said, well, hell, Barkley, you love her too. And I do. It's like I've waited for you to, I don't know, catch up with me. Being my friend first was special. We have talked so much about ourselves that I feel that loving you is the next step. Our next step."

"I'm not going back home. I feel that here is where I need to be. To be with you. I'd like to talk my brothers into staying here as well so that they're close, but I don't know that they will. I think that Robert and Dan would stay forever if they find the right home to live in." He took a couple of steps toward her when she did the same. "Falling in love with you, Barkley, wasn't at all what I thought would happen between us. Or anyone, for that matter. It was so soft, the love that came to me for you. Soft and right. Like you said, our hearts needed to catch up with how we feel."

"Will you marry me?" She nodded, and he felt like he'd be able to take on the world at that moment. "I don't have a ring on me for you, but I do have one. Believe it or not, but I only just sent it to be cleaned at the jeweler this morning. I got it back this afternoon, and it's upstairs in the jewelry box. It's a wedding band set. I saw it there yesterday where my cufflinks are and thought that I'd show it to you. But then I realized that it was dirty, grimy, I guess you could call it." They were standing toe to toe now, and he reached out to touch his fingers to her cheek. Then her hair. "Your hair is as silky as I thought it would be. Beautiful. And your eyes are such a beautiful shade of blue that I can't help but think that artist and painters would be looking for a way to capture the color to paint something with it."

"I can't wait to have your child, Barkley. I hope that our sons look like you." He leaned down and kissed her gently on the lips and then on her jawline and ears. "You're making me insane here. My brothers are in the house, or I'd tell you to take me right here on the floor."

"I think we can do better than that." Barkley

picked her up in his arms, realizing how light she was and was slightly afraid of breaking her. As he headed up the stairs to his room, he yelled out to Dan and Robert to go away. He could hear them laughing as the front door opened and closed. "Now. We're all alone in the house. What would you like for me to do to you first? I'm hard and up for anything you might want to do."

They were both laughing as they stripped their clothes off. While kissing her, he got his arm caught up in his shirt from the cufflinks he'd had on today. He made a decision right then that he wasn't going to wear them anymore so long as he didn't have to. Barkley even decided that he was going to start dressing down. He had to think if he even owned a pair of blue jeans or a T-shirt.

"You are wearing too many clothes." He told her what he'd been thinking while she undid his cufflink. "Good. And you need some shorts too. Something more than the ones that your grandda wears. Why does he need all those pockets?"

"He told me once that he was forever carrying granny's things so she'd not have to carry her purse everywhere. So it's a habit that he couldn't break. Christ, you're beautiful." He'd gotten her blouse off and then her bra. With just her panties on, he could see that she was simply perfect in every way. And she was his.

Taking several deep breaths before he touched her, Barkley was afraid of hurting her in some way. She seemed so fragile, so tiny. Even though she was nearly as tall as he was, he didn't see her that way. All he could see was that everything about her said she was too tiny for him. When she laughed, he asked her what she was thinking about.

"You. You grumble when you're thinking. I'm not at all tiny, Barkley. I'm a grown assed woman that needs to be fucked like she's never been fucked before." He grinned at her. "Do you understand the assignment? You're to fuck me and make me come so many times that I pass out?"

"Yes. I'll do you one better. I'll make it so that we both pass out. How does that sound to you?" She leapt into his arms and wrapped her legs around his waist. "You're so right. You're not too tiny for me."

He suckled at her breasts and made love to her

mouth with his own. She tasted of the peaches that she'd had for lunch. The sweet taste was sexy and tantalizing to him. When she began riding him, her body moving up and down over his, Barkley took her to the bed and laid down atop of her. He stood up and pulled his pants off, along with his boxers.

"I never thought that I'd say this, but you certainly make boxers look fucking sexy." Barkley didn't know what to say to her, so he simply smiled at her again. "I love you, Barkley. But if you don't take me right now, I'm going to hurt you badly. Understand?"

"I do. I was just thinking about where I wanted to start." He got down on his knees and between her legs. "I think I'd like to start right here. Where I can smell you the best. And you do smell fantastic."

Barkley made a feast of her pussy. Nibbling on her clit, his mouth was flooded with her cream. Each time she cried out that she was coming, he paused just enough so that she'd not. It was a dangerous way to play with her, but he wanted her to enjoy this as much as he did. And teasing her seemed to be just what they both wanted.

Sliding his fingers into her sheath, Carrie nearly

bucked him off when she came hard. Her screams filled the room and his ears. Lapping up her climax with his tongue, he felt it drip from his hand to his cock. Nearly sending him into space when he touched his cock with his free hand.

Slowly he slid his hand up and down his cock. The precum at the tip was giving him just enough to make the slide easy. His balls hurt; they were so full, and all he wanted to do was to come. Carrie jerked his head up from her body, and he stared at her. She was the most beautiful creature he'd ever seen.

"Fuck me." He told her he wasn't finished tasting her just yet. "You're finished right now if you don't. I mean it. Please, Barkley. I need you to come inside of me. It's all that is holding me together right now. The thought of you coming deep inside of me."

He stood up, and she leaned up and licked his cock. Holding onto his balls as they ached with a fullness he'd never felt before, he nearly came all over Carrie when she spread her legs wide for him and begged him again to take her.

Pulling her up off the bed by her legs, she wrapped her legs around him as he filled her. She cried out, screaming his name and begging for more. Taking her to the wall, he pressed her against it and fucked her hard and without mercy.

Barkley savagely took her mouth. Biting her lower lip, he continued to take her. When she threw back her head and cried out again, he watched her face though he didn't stop taking her. He wasn't even sure if he could have. Her beauty and her uninhibited abandonment way she was enjoying each stroke of his cock, made him fall in love with her again and again.

Carrie dug her nails into his back. Nearly passing out with the pain-pleasure of it, he let himself go. Giving her what she wanted too, as he emptied his cock and balls into her so hard that he knew for sure that he was going to be sore for a year after this.

Barkley came twice more, his body spent and nearly hanging on as he held her pressed against the wall. He'd lost count of how many times she'd come. Her voice, he figured, would be as sore as his when she spoke again from the way she had been so vocal about her release.

Each time Carrie moved, even if she only took in a deeper breath, his cock would jerk, and he'd ache again. But for whatever reason, it wasn't a pain that he didn't want to repeat. It was wonderful how her body made his feel.

Lifting his head up to look at her when she told him she was getting a cramp in her leg, he willed his body to the bed, where he simply dropped onto it. He knew that, on some level that he needed to move off of her, but his body just shut down. Barkley was spent. Not only that, but he'd felt the most profound sense of happiness that he didn't think he'd felt before.

When she cried out, waking him, he sat up on the bed and helped her with the cramp in her leg. Neither of them said a word, but he could tell that she was just as exhausted as he was. When she grinned at him after lying back on the bed, he asked her what she was thinking.

"Remind me never to challenge you about sex again. You're a killer." That made his chest swell with the compliment. "Also, you understood the assignment and finished up at the top of your class. I might not ever be the same again."

"Before I forget." Like a fool, he stood up and started for his dresser when he fell to the floor. Instead of helping him up, like he thought that she should have done, Carrie was laughing so hard that he finally told her that he wasn't going to give her the ring that he'd picked up this afternoon while the wedding bands were being cleaned. She told him to get up. "You're very mean when you're sated. Has anyone ever told you that before?"

"I've only just realized that I've never been sated before if this is what it feels like. Christ, I think I could get used to this feeling." Barkley told her that he'd not last very long if they made love like this daily. "True. I never thought about that."

Getting up off the floor, he made his way to the dresser. He would swear that it moved back away from him several feet for each step he took. Making his way back to the bed, he was a little more energetic as he couldn't wait to see his ring on her finger.

"I love you, Carrie Boone. Will you be my wife?" She told him she'd already told him yes downstairs but asked him if he was going to propose properly to her. "If you want the entire thing, like me getting down on one knee, you're going to be disappointed. I can barely walk as it is. But I do love you."

Barkley put the ring on her finger, and it fit as if it had been made just for her. If he didn't know better, he'd swear that it looked better on her hand than it did on his granny's when she'd worn it before passing away. He told her where the ring had come from.

"It was my mom's mother's ring. We were never close. Not any of us boys were close to her. She was a stickler for people doing the right thing. Rules were her friends." Carrie asked him if she'd been mean to them as boys. "Not mean. But she was difficult to get to know all that well. We were only allowed to hug her when she'd put a towel on her dress first. She would talk to us nicely, but she was never one for physical contact. I think that's why my mom loves to hug people when she meets them. Dad, too, I think. He told me once that Grannie Wilson was a nice old lady, but he thought that she'd been old long before her time. I didn't understand that until I was older and watched my other grannie getting around."

"You're very lucky to have all your family around you. I do have my brothers, but I was young when our parents died. They raised me. By then, Robert was almost twenty-one and in a relationship with

Dan. The others, my brothers, weren't hard on me, but they did make sure that I was well cared for and got a good education." He said he could tell. "Thanks." She smiled at him when she laid her head on his chest as he got back into bed. "I'm going to go and see Mick tomorrow. I just want some answers about my sister. Like, did she ever mention us? Did she ever try to get in touch with any of us? I don't think that she did, but I'd like to know if he has the reason for her not being a part of our lives."

"Just be careful." She told him that she would be. "I'm going to have to go and inspect some land tomorrow that we're thinking of purchasing. Want me to reschedule it?"

"No. I'm going to be in a police station with a lot of armed officers around. I think I'll be just fine." Barkley was sure that she would be, but he also didn't want her to be hurt. Mentally nor physically. "I'm going to tell my brothers where I'm going so that if I come up missing, they'll know where to start looking."

"That's not funny." She laughed at him for a good hour as they dressed and made their way downstairs to find something to munch on. He was glad that Robert and Dan had started dinner and left out things they could eat. Barkley suddenly found himself starved.

Chapter 6

Mick couldn't stand being in the cell next to his fathers. It was one of the main reasons that he'd moved out of the family home when he'd been old enough. His father was a pervert and a bastard. It wasn't until spending time next to him like this that Mick realized that he hated him. And more than likely had for most of his life.

Mick could hear his father when he made the slightest moves or when he passed gas. He made no apologies for it but laughed. Especially at night. The fucking bastard would jack off twice a night and call out his daughters' names. It was sickening, and he wanted to crawl through the bars and beat him until he was dead. It was all he could do on most nights not to throw up all over himself.

"You're being moved." He looked at the officer standing in front of him. He'd not heard him come up to the cell. He'd been thinking so hard about how to get into his dad's cell and kill him. "Gather your stuff up and follow me, Cartwright."

"Where are we going?" Turning, Mick nearly snarled at his father to shut up. He was the one being spoken to when the officer said that it was only him that was moving. He had forever done that. Answered questions that had been put to him or just thinking that everything revolved around him. "No. No, I won't have that. I need my son here. We've lost so much together, and I want him right here where I can console him when he needs it. Besides, we have to make plans for when the two of us get out of here. There are those babies that need to be brought home so that—"

"You're not moving. It's just him. I'm doing just what I was told, so you sit there and keep your trap shut." He didn't bother telling his father goodbye or even telling him that he'd talk to them about moving him too. Mick was out the door and with the officer before anyone charged their minds. They were nearly to the front of the place where the cells were when he spoke again. "You're going to be on the B wing for the rest of your stay here."

He hadn't any idea what that meant. They had wings in this jailhouse? When they were rounding the corner of the hallway they were on, he noticed a young woman sitting in a chair next to a cell. When he was put inside the cell she was near, she didn't move but watched as he was told his cell number as well as his new schedule for his food trays. It was going to be ten minutes earlier than before. Once the officer left him, not saying a word about the woman, Mick stared at her. It occurred to him who she might well be.

"You're related to Mattie. Her sister, I'm thinking. Not that you look all that much like her, but you do have the same brilliant blue eyes." She said she was her younger sister, Carrie Boone. "I saw you the other day. When you were with one of the Strong men."

"Yes. Barkley Strong. He was protecting me from you. Last night he asked me to marry him." He could see it then, the shiny ring on her finger. If it was a diamond, it was one of the largest ones he'd ever seen. "I came here to talk to you about Mattie and what happened to her the years that she left us. You don't have to talk to me if you don't want to. I understand that the two of you had made a life together and —"

"The twins, they're not mine." If he meant to shock her, he couldn't tell by her expression. "They're my fathers. I can't have children. I mean, I can't even get my dick to be — I'm sorry. I don't mean to be so crude, but I had a botched-up circumcision when I was nineteen, and I can't have sex, much less father children. I needed to get it done when my parents started talking about grandchildren. I couldn't let that happen."

"So Maddie had an affair with your father that produced the children. Is that the main reason that your mother killed her?" He said that Mom was all right with the two of them having an affair. Sometimes she'd join them. "That's fucking sick."

"Tell me about it." He looked around and then back at her. "I'd like to talk to you. To confess, I guess. Also, I don't know what is going to happen to me, but I'd like to make it so that my father can't get to the girls. He'll kill them if he keeps raping them. And he is.

I'm afraid of my father — not just afraid but terrified of him. What he'll do to me once this is over and — he has all these plans now that my wife and mother are gone. He wants me to live with him with the girls so that he can be around them all the time. He's a sick bastard, and I can't stand to be with or around him anymore." Mick sobbed then.

He'd been holding it all in since he'd been a child, and it was getting the best of him now, not just with his father but with the things that were coming to him now from his childhood. There wasn't any way that he was going to survive living with his father. Carrie asked him if he was all right. He nodded then she spoke again.

"What do you mean, confess?" He shrugged and looked up at the camera that had a glowing bright red light on the side of it. "They told me that you were aware of being recorded all the time. It records sound as well."

"Yes, I'm aware of it." He looked at her. "I want to confess everything that I know about my parents and my wife, Mattie. I'm no saint in all of the things that have happened. I'm well aware, too, that by not reporting the things that they did, it makes me just as guilty. And I did help with some of the things that my father did. I want to tell you all of it. If I had a gun, I'd use it on myself rather than to tell anyone what happened, but I think that it needs to be told, the story of my parents and Mattie." He laughed a little. "I might well have used one a long time ago had I had access to a gun."

She didn't say anything to him about his attempt at humor. He wasn't entirely sure that it was humor and more the truth than he'd ever expressed before. Once he settled himself on his cot after moving it closer to Carrie, he laid down. She didn't say anything as he began talking to her. Or to himself. He wasn't sure which, but he knew that he'd been holding onto it for far too long now.

"Before I start talking, I want you to know that I've kept journals all my life. Since I was old enough to put sentences together. I've kept them in my room under the floorboards until I left home. Then when I got myself a place of my own, I had a safe put in the floor so that no one would be able to get to them. There are hundreds of them under there. So when you go to get them, make sure that you take someone with you. I want you to use them to make sure that my father is found out." She told him that she'd do that. Mick not only gave her the combination to the safe, but he also told her about the map. "It shows where all the bodies are hidden. At least those that I was there when they were killed and buried. I have the longitude and latitude of each place there with their names and the reason that they were killed. I will admit that I had killed two of the people there. My father wanted me to have a part in it so that I'd know what it felt like to end the life of a person. I don't think I got the joy of it that he was hoping for. He nearly beat me to death when I threw up after killing the first person."

"Your parents are sick fucks. I hope you know that." He said that he did. More than she did. "I guess. I do have a question before you begin. The day that Mattie was killed. Why did she die if your father was having an affair with her?"

"He loved her. I mean, like he did my mother. In fact, he was having an affair with her long before I married her. It was the reason that I was told I had to marry her. So that he could conduct his affairs without anyone knowing about them. I don't know why he cared. I think everyone in the town knew that they were in a relationship. Their love, it was strong too. I think because they were so much alike. My mom loved her too." He thought about the time he'd walked in on his mother and wife in bed together and shivered. "They were lovers too. The two of them. It wasn't until Mattie lost her first child that things started to change with her. She became…I guess you'd call it unstable. More so than before."

Mick explained to Carrie that Mattie had been pregnant three times before the girls had been born. Each time she lost a child, she would get more and more unstable. It wasn't until she passed the six month of carrying the girls that she started to behave like a normal person.

"Well, as normal as she could be, I guess. She'd always had a little bit of an emotional problem. Not just with depression, she'd been seeing someone for that, but Mattie couldn't contain her emotions from one second to the next. No matter how many different combinations of drugs she was put on." He remembered what Carrie had asked him. "After the girls were born, Mattie started acting out. Beating the girls for no reason. It got to the point where I'd not allow her to be around them. When I had to go away for a day even, I'd take them to my parents' home. Then one day, I went to pick the girls up, and there was blood in their diapers. My mother told me that it was my father who had done it, that he'd been having a bit of fun with them. Like he did with me when I was little. I hadn't remembered that until then. My dad and my mother raped me when I was a baby until I was about five years old."

"It's a small wonder that you survived for as long as you have." He told her it wasn't for lack of trying to end his life. "I'm sorry to hear that. I truly am."

Mick wasn't sure why, but he believed her. That she truly did feel bad for him. As he told her about the plan to end Maddie's life, she asked a few questions about the death of his mom. Why had she been there to be killed by the police.

"She wasn't supposed to die. Not that my father cared all that much when he found out. The plan that had been set was messed up when the Strong man, Barkley, I guess now, came up upon the two of them.

Mattie was nearly dead by then, just the way it was supposed to have happened. Mom was supposed to leave the area, and then Dad would have paid off the police to have them leave things the way that they were. Mattie had been killed by some unknown person, and that would have been the end of it. The story was that Mattie was unstable and had provoked my mom into killing her was going to be the story. The police arrived before she was able to leave, thanks to Barkley calling the police too soon for Mom to escape. So I guess she figured that she was a Cartwright and that the police wouldn't harm her. Dad, he told me that he was glad for the way that things ended up. With them both dead, myself and the girls could move in with him, and it would be just fine and dandy." He thought about the things that had happened that day. "The reason that my dad told me not to allow an autopsy was because he'd been poisoning Mattie since the babies had been born. But it was taking too long for him, and he hatched this plan to have her killed."

"Did it bother you that an—I was going to say an innocent person was killed, but she wasn't, was she? Mattie was just as sick as the rest of them were." Mick said that, at times, she was worse than his father. "I never knew Mattie. By the time that I was born and old enough to realize that she was my sister, she was gone. It had been decades since any of us had heard from her, and when our parents died, we didn't know how to get in touch with her to let her know."

"She more than likely wouldn't have cared. Mattie was forever complaining that her parents and the rest of you were keeping her under a tight thumb. I don't know what that meant, but as you can imagine, I did understand why they did it. Mattie might well have had something wrong with her when she was born. I believe that." He thought about something. "I'm going to sign the paperwork to have her autopsy done. Also, anything else they want to do to her. As my mother's son, if I can, I'm going to allow the police to do what they need to for my mother too. I know that she wasn't nearly as bad as Mattie, but they were two peas in a pod about so many different things."

"You'll need an attorney." He said that he wanted to use someone that wasn't anyone that his father knew. "You think that he'd tell him what you're doing? That he'd do something to make it so that it never happens?"

"I'm positive of that." He laid there for several minutes without speaking. Thinking of the life he'd had. "I'd like for you to adopt the girls. Now, if you can. It would make me feel better knowing that when my dad is able to get out of this mess, he won't be the one that has them."

"You think that he'll be able to make a case that has him free? I don't see how that is going to happen, not with all the things that you've told me." Mick told her that his father was good at getting out of anything he set his mind to. "Well, I'm going to enjoy him going down more than I thought I would have. He's going to pay for the crimes that he's committed, and I'm going to be there when he gets his comeuppance."

"I hope that you're right." She made a couple of calls on his behalf and arranged for an attorney to come to him. While she was making the calls, Mick could hear his father down at the other end of the corridor yelling about him being next to him. And most importantly, to keep his mouth shut or else. For some reason, the or else didn't scare him as much as it normally would have.

He was talking about things that made no sense now that he was away from him. That they were family and deserved to be together. Perhaps in the same cell. Mick had a sudden thought that if they were in the same cell, he'd never come out of there alive. His father would kill him just so he'd be able to get his daughters. It was something that he couldn't nor would allow to happen. Not so long as he had breath in his body, he wouldn't.

~*~

Barkley only had to sign the paperwork as a witness then things would be set in motion for Mattie and Jane Cartwright. The attorney for Mick had had everything drawn up for the other man in two days and then to have it signed. He looked at Mick when he said his name.

"I can get someone else to witness my signature if you'd like." Barkley told him that it wasn't that. But he was curious why he was doing this. Now of all times. "I don't want to die with all this on my chest. Mostly it's to get Bethany and Sunny into a good home. One that isn't perverted by my family. I don't know you all that well, nor your family, but everyone that is working here has said that your family is one of the best there is. You'd take the shirt off your back to give it to someone if they needed it."

Barkley had read the contract over at home and knew that it was more in his and Carrie's favor than Mick's, so he signed his name where it was required, and Mick did the same. When the attorney left, he asked if he could talk to Mick for a little while. That he had questions of his own.

"Yes, of course. After talking to Carrie, I feel like I'm finally doing something right for a change. Getting my heart in the right place for the girls has been taken care of by the two of you. Thank you for that." Barkley asked why he'd never gone to the police. "I was terrified of my father. Still am, to be honest. Also, he had the police department as well as all the attorneys there in his pocket. Things either went his way, or he'd be burying them in the land around his home. Did you find the map?"

"Yes. The FBI is working on that. Also, with the information you gave us on the town's police officers, they've been fired and arrested too. I think Carrie told you that." He said that she had. "Good. I wanted to ask you what you think to gain from all this? For giving Carrie the girls? For telling on your father? Do you expect to be some kind of hero after this comes out? I don't mean to be rude here, but you have to have a reason for doing this."

"I do. Not one that I completely understand myself. I want to unburden myself about my parents mostly. As for being a hero? No, I know I've slipped too far down the way to Hell to ever be anything but what I am now. A man that let his father abuse his daughters. Myself too, but it was my girls that got me thinking that I need to do something." Barkley asked if he had allowed it. "No. I wouldn't have ever done that. But now it's too late. They've both been hurt, and it's my fault too. As you said, I should have said something to someone to make it stop. But I didn't. I'm working on making it better for them, much better than I had it when I was a child. But that's not good enough because it did happen, and in some way, I allowed it to happen to them."

The two of them talked about the other things that had been mentioned in the paperwork that the attorney had set up. There was insurance money that hadn't been cashed in that was on Mattie, which was his. Also, there was money in his accounts as well as the houses that he'd purchased with the thought of running away to one of them.

"It would never be far enough. I think I always knew that. I told myself that with each new purchase of land that I'd get, I'd be able to hide there if I needed to. Mattie never knew about the money or the places. I'm sure that my father had an idea that I was putting together a place where I could be safe. Mother was oblivious to everything that didn't have to do with spending money and hosting stupid parties." Mick laughed. "Sell it all, as I did mention in the things that I have for the girls. Or not. Use it in any way that you wish. The only thing that I'm going to ask you is that you don't paint a too horrific picture of me to them. No way will they ever be a part of my life again, but I don't want them to think I didn't try in the end."

"My dad is going to see about getting you into a prison that isn't one that your father is going to be in. He said that with your help and cooperation, it wouldn't be too hard to convince a judge to do that for you." Mick started crying. He told him that he would be ever so grateful if he were to get that for him. "I'll make sure that when Dad knows anything, I'll let you know. But as I said, it shouldn't be a problem."

It was nearly ten in the morning, nine forty-five, when he left to go to the courthouse on the Chase matter. Barkley had been working on this case since he'd first been approached by Chase to buy the land off of him. Once he started digging, he found out all sorts of things about the older man. Too many for him to think that the man was going to be spending the rest of his life in prison.

John Chase had been trying to sell his sister's land that she inherited from their mother. Since finding out that he'd not just killed off his parents and siblings, but also had a hand in the death of his sister's husband, Barkley was excited to see this all go down. Elizabeth Chase-Brown was about ten years older than her brother. But she was a great deal smarter. Today her daughter, Tessa Jane Chase-Brown, was coming to town to hear what the courts had to say about her uncle. Apparently there was bad blood between the two of them as well.

"Mr. Strong?" He nodded and took the hand of

the younger woman. "I'm Tessa. My mom is on her way, but she's running late. She doesn't get around as well as she used to and has to wait on her meds to kick in before she can leave her room."

"She is a wonderful person, your mom." Tessa brightened up and said that she was the best. "You know all that is going to be said today, correct? About how your uncle murdered your father and your grandfather?"

"I told Mom that he'd done it. He figures, for whatever reason, that my dad would have left him in charge of his estate and my mom and me when he was gone. Instead, Dad not only left nothing to his brother-in-law, but he also mentioned that he thought that Uncle John was a fool and would hurt anyone who got in his way about money. As you can imagine, that didn't go over all that well." Tessa laughed. "My mom is a good deal smarter than he is, and every time he tried his shit, she'd knock him back a few steps. I would, too, when I was old enough to take care of myself. John is a bastard and a murderer, and I'm thrilled to see him going down for his activities."

"Hopefully, we'll be able to keep him in jail

while the time for the trial is set up. It could be another month if there is nothing open soon." She said that she worked from home, and it didn't matter where she was. But she was going to stick it out until he was out of their hair. "Your mom told me that you're a voice artist. I didn't think to ask her what that meant."

"I read books on tape for people. Also, when I can, I do voice-overs for cartoons and such. Twice I've been the voice of an actress that had a cold and couldn't get her voice to work well enough. No one seemed to notice the difference." Barkley told her that sounded like fun. "It can be. Sometimes it gets a little hairy when I don't care for the book I'm reading, but I get it done. It pays the bills, and I like it. Which is a win-win for me."

Her mom, Elizabeth, showed up just as they were getting settled into their seats. Elizabeth decided that she was going to sit up front with him, and she wanted Tessa there as well. He didn't mind. All his paperwork was in order, and all he wanted to do was get this thing in the books so that he could send the man off to jail. Then they brought in John.

To say that he didn't do well in jail was an

understatement. His hair was stringy and needed a good scrub, it looked to Barkley. John didn't have a suit on, which surprised him but the jailhouse greens that all inmates wore after a couple of days. His eye was blackened, and he looked as if his hands were bruised. While he had no idea how that had happened, he did think that whatever caused it had been John's fault.

As soon as John sat in one of the chairs at the other table, Judge Marshall called things to order. Then he asked him what they were there for today. It was John that spoke up before he could.

"My sister stole my inheritance from me. That's what is going on." The judge looked at him as John continued. "She somehow talked my mother into leaving everything to her, and I'm betting now that she was supposed to give it to me so that I can manage it. Women have no head for money, and I have a deal that will make me — err, us millions." The judge asked him if that was true.

"No, your honor. Mrs. Brown was the sole heir to her mother's estate. There was no mention that Mr. Chase was to receive anything as she felt that he's stolen enough from her while she was alive. She mentioned in her will that she believed that John, her son, had murdered his father and brothers." Chase said he'd done no such thing. "I have the revised death certificates of Theodore Chase and John's three younger brothers — deceased. After exhuming their bodies, it was found that they had all been given a lethal dose of fentanyl just hours before they passed."

Barkley handed the paperwork to the judge and then to the attorney for Chase. John wouldn't even look at it when his attorney handed it to him. As he went on to talk about the death of the husband of Elizabeth, having the same cause of death, the judge looked at John.

"Not only does Mr. Strong here have you for trying to sell property that didn't belong to you, but he's also dug up some very damning information on the deaths of a few family members as well. What do you have to say for yourself, Mr. Chase?" He asked if he had any proof that he supposedly did this. "Mr. Strong?"

"When the police entered the home of Mr. Chase, they found several prescription pads from a doctor that has been deceased for a number of years with his signature printed on them. I don't believe they are able to do that anymore. But all of the prescriptions that had been filled on those pads had been bought and paid for by Mr. John Chase. He would be required to sign his name that he'd picked them up. Also, I've talked to the pharmacies around the area where he would get them filled, and there are receipts for all of them being filled for fentanyl. Over two hundred scripts were filled for Mr. Chase over the last eight years." The judge asked if he'd heard him right. "Yes, sir. Over two hundred of them. As you can imagine, the pharmacies are being investigated for filling them without checking to see that the doctor in question had been deceased for fourteen years by then."

"I had a good thing going there, too, until he put his ass in the way. Do you have any idea how much you can make off of one pill of fentanyl? Why I can get upwards of five grand for just a couple of pounds of the shit. More if it's in a place where they're rich people wanting them." The judge asked him to be quiet. "I will not. I want this over with too. I have shit to do, and being in here is not allowing me to get busy with it. My sister isn't smart enough to have our parents' land. Besides, what is it? Twenty or so acres. Christ, I'm getting four million for it when this is over. I think that alone is worth it for her to keep her trap shut about me not owning it."

"Twenty acres?" Tessa looked at her uncle and smiled. "You've no idea what you're talking about. Not only are there one hundred acres here in town, but there are twenty thousand acres on the ranch out west. More than that in Texas as well. You selling it for a sum of four million wouldn't even make a small dent in what all that land is really worth. Christ, you're dumber than I first thought."

"You should know better than to talk to me that way. You hear me?" Tessa just flipped him off, and Barkley burst out laughing. So did Judge Marshall. But then he caught himself and told Tessa to keep her language clean. She grinned at the judge and told him that she was sorry. Barkley didn't think that neither he nor the judge believed a word that she said.

Chapter 7

Carrie waited until the judge called the room to order before she stood up. Having notes on what she was to say was helpful. More than anything, she wanted this to work out the way that she wanted it to. Careful planning had gone into this one moment.

"Ms. Boone?" She nodded to the judge and asked if she could come to the front. "Does this have to do with the pretrial that is going to happen in a few minutes? If so, can it not wait?"

"No, your honor, I'm afraid that it can't. You're bringing in both Mr. Michael Cartwright and his son Mick Cartwright together, and I'd like to ask you something before they enter the room. Please?" He nodded, and she moved to the front of the room. "I believe you've been made aware of Mick's help in getting all the bodies found on his father's land, correct?"

"Yes. There were forty-three of them, if memory serves. The Feds were also given a book kept by Mr. Cartwright on the names as well as the supposed crime that happened that put them there. All good information." She told him that they found one more just last night, so the count was forty-four. "All right. So it's forty-four. What does that have to do with these proceedings?"

"I would like to ask if it's possible that Mr. Mick Cartwright be given a much lighter sentence than would be normal for the crimes that he committed." She handed him a file that she'd been working on for the past three days. "There you have Mick's medical records, as well as the psychiatric profile that was done on behalf of the courtroom today. If you'll notice, the doctor said that with his childhood trauma as well as the harm done to his daughters, it's small wonder that Mick is terrified of his father."

"I read that last night. I don't know that I would

have been able to be composed daily if those things had happened to me." She said that she knew that she wouldn't have. "I have the paperwork on his wife as well as the DNA tests on the children. They're Michael Cartwright's children."

"Yes. But Mick has taken care of them—well as best he could under the circumstances of living with the three of them. I believe, as well as the doctor that has examined them, that it is small wonder that they survived living around their grandparents and mother." The judge asked her if she had something she was getting to. "I do, your honor. In addition to Mick having a much lighter sentence than his father, I'd like to request that he be in an entirely different time zone from his father. He believes as do I and my brothers believe, that Michael will kill Mick because he'll find out during this trial that he's the one that had been helping the police."

"I do believe that you're right. And as much as I'd like to agree with you that it would work out for him to be put someplace safe, he won't be. It won't matter how—I've looked over the testimony that came with the paperwork for today, and Mr. Michael has a long arm that gets him what he wants. It won't matter where either of them is situated. He'll somehow get word to someone to have his son killed." She told him she didn't want that. "I don't either, after having a talk with him last night."

"I didn't know that you've spoken to him." He winked at her. "You're a good man, Judge Marshall. What you did for the Brown women was well above what anyone could have asked for. And to have their relative put in solitary confinement for the rest of his life was a stroke of genius if you asked me."

"Are you, by any chance buttering me up, Ms. Boone?" She felt her face heat up and said that no one had ever accused her of doing that before. "No. I've spoken to your future father-in-law and Barkley. You're more of a get right to the meat of things sort of woman."

"Yes, sir, I am." She looked around the room. "I was going to ask you if it would be possible that Mick serve no time. He's a good man and has helped the United States put a very-very bad man behind bars. He's given up a lot for that, including his own safety."

"Ms. Boone, I like you. However, it is my

understanding that Mick, as you call him, committed murder twice. The people that he killed, you don't think that their loved ones deserve justice for their deaths?" She told him what she thought. "I suppose you could be right. That they were happy just to have closure of finally putting their loved ones to rest. But he did do the crime."

"I have statements from the two families, your honor." He said something like *of course you* do, but she chose to ignore it. "They are thrilled to have their family members back, and they wouldn't have gotten that without his help. Also, insurance policies were cashed now that they had a body. At a much-needed time too. The money that they're getting will go a long way in putting their children through college and keeping food on the table."

"You should have been a lawyer, my dear. I wish someone fought this hard for me when my missus is upset." Carrie told him what to do. "Yes, I suppose that would help matters if I were to bring her home roses and candy once in a while, but she'd wonder what I'd done."

"Good. Keeping her on her toes is good too.

Don't you think?" He laughed with her. "I think that if anyone deserves a second chance at life, it would be Mick. While you're thinking on that, sir, Mick will need a new identity too, sir. So that he's safe."

"He won't have anything to do with his daughters? Or his half-sisters, I guess?" She told him that she had adopted them legally and that as soon as she and Barkley were married, he'd adopt them as well. Also, he'd turned over all his worldly goods so that the girls wouldn't have to worry about anything. "I would imagine that they'd not have to anyway being adopted by a Strong. But I do see your point. Let me think on this for a bit. In the meantime, I'm going to call a recess for half an hour. Do you believe that you can wait that long, young lady?"

"Yes, sir. I can. I know that you'll do the right thing by all those innocent lives." She went back to her seat only to stand up once more and address the judge. Her brothers all stood up with their wives when she stood this time. "Your honor, if you allow it, this is the support team that Mick will have along with the Strongs. We'll all make sure that he has everything he needs when he's put someplace safe and that even though we won't see him, he'll know that all he has to do is call, and we'll all help him. Mick, for all that has happened to him, is a good man. And one that I'm proud to call a brother-in-law."

Her brothers said the same. That they were proud of the things that Mick had done to make sure that not only was his father held accountable for his crimes but that his sisters were safe as well.

It was well past the thirty-minute mark, and she was getting nervous. She didn't know what was going on behind those closed doors, but having her brothers there with her and Barkley too, she thought that she was handling things well.

"You all right?" She told Barkley that she'd be better once this was done. "Yeah, I think all of us will. What do you suppose is going on in his office? I mean, it's kind of scary that it's taking longer than he said it would."

"I know. Why don't you tell me what happened with the Chase hearing? I know you started to tell me once, but then we got sidetracked. Not that I'm complaining, but what happened there?" He kissed her on the nose, and she felt better. "You're very good at distracting me, you know that, don't you?"

"That's the plan. Mr. Chase was sent to prison when he tried to kill Tessa. Who I like, by the way." She told him that she did as well. "Anyway, he's gotten life without parole. Which is good for a great many people. He'll also be in solitary confinement too. Only able to get out and about for thirty minutes twice a day. Tessa and her mom are going to stay here for a while. They're going to donate the land here in town to the Strong Foundation and help with the houses that are going to be built on the land for first-time home buyers. It's a good cause and one that my family is willing to get behind."

"So he got nothing anyway." Barkley told her that was right. "Stupid man. Why on earth did he think that he could have gotten away with that? I mean, did he actually think that everyone was going to be just fine with him selling his sister's land for much less than it was worth? Not only that, but to have murdered people to get what he wanted? He must have been dropped on his head a lot as a child. If I were his parent, I would have kept dropping him until he was out of my hair. He's a monster."

An hour later, they were called back into the courtroom. The judge looked like he'd gone a couple of rounds with a fighter and had lost. Carrie wondered what had happened in the time they'd been gone. The bailiff came to stand next to them when the judge was seated. As soon as he was, she was handed an envelope and told to open it. She looked at the judge, and he winked at her. Michael was brought in, but there was no sign of Mick. The judge began speaking as she was getting the letter out.

"There has been an accident, I'm afraid." Judge Marshall looked at Michael. "I'm sorry to tell you this, sir, but your son was killed twenty minutes ago when he tried to escape from custody. So because of this, we're going to delay this pretrial for two weeks while—"

"What do you mean, he was killed? I just spoke to him an hour ago." The judge asked Michael if he remembered what they had spoken about. "Yes. I told him that I was going to get us both out of this stupid mess and that we'd be going home. My son...he's really dead?"

"I'm afraid so." Michael stood up and put out his

hands. He asked to be released. "I'm sorry? What do you mean, you want to be released? The trial will still go on as planned but only delayed."

"No. That isn't going to work for me. I have daughters to raise. Especially in light of their father being gone, they'll need me to take care of them. I want you to take these outrageous cuffs off of me so I can raise those little girls as I should have been able to do all alone." Carrie stood up. She told the courtroom, as she had been told to do in the letter, that she and her husband—arranged and taken care of by Judge Marshall—had adopted the children. "You have no right to do that? They're mine."

"They were my sister's daughters, so I, as well as the rest of my family here, will raise them as our own. I think that under the circumstances, they're better off with me than you, you sick bastard." He lunged at her but didn't do anything but tangle himself up in his cuffs. "Not only will they be safe, but they'll have a good life without you being there."

"You can't let this happen to them or me. They're mine. I want them to live with me." The judge told him to sit down and shut up. "I will not. What will it take to make things right for me? I have money. As soon as I get the insurance check from my wife's death, I'll sign that over to you. Come on, everyone has a price. Name it."

"You just tried to bribe me. Are you aware of that?" Michael told Judge Marshall that he did it all the time, and no one had yet to turn him down. Not if they were smart. "Yes, I can understand how that would work out for you. I believe that two of the bodies that were dug up on your land were judges of good standing."

"What the ever-loving fuck are you doing digging around on my land? You stop that right now. Damn it. What is the world coming to when a man's land isn't safe from people like you? Whatever you found, I didn't put them there." The judge pulled out a sheet of paper and began reading off the names of the dead as well as how they were killed and why. "Where did you — that mother fucking little shit. Mick did this to me, didn't he? He was so against me raising my daughters that he told on me. Did he also tell you that he killed some of them too? The pussy had to be made to kill them. He was so squeamish about it. Christ. If he wasn't dead already, I'd kill him myself."

"Are you telling me that you forced your son to kill those people? What sort of threat did you use?" Michael seemed not to understand that he was confessing to crimes that would get him into trouble. He even told the judge how he'd had to help Mick hold the gun and pull the trigger on the first body. "I've heard enough."

The judge sat there for several minutes as he seemed lost in thought. Carrie could tell that he was angry. When Andrew poked her, she handed him the letter. In it was the perfect lifesaver for Mick Cartwright.

Mick wasn't dead. That had been written in bold letters across the top of the letter to them. But he had been made to look like he was. After pictures were taken of him being killed and he was whisked away, Mick was on his way to a better, much safer life. The judge also told her to make sure that they didn't contact him as he'd been taken care of by Barkley and Lisa Strong and would want for nothing. There was also mention of the insurance policy that had belonged to Mick. It would come to the babies as well.

"Mr. Cartwright, I don't know why I was

surprised by your lack of feelings for the death of your only son. Be that as it may, I am going to sentence you now and save the taxpayers a great deal of money. I think that taking you to trial would indeed be a waste of time, as you mentioned earlier." He thanked him. "You might want to take that back in a few minutes. I'm sentencing you to fifty years for each of the bodies found on your property. An additional five hundred years for the sodomy of your children. Which would include—" Michael told him that wasn't going to work for him. That he needed out. "I don't give a good god damn, you monster. This is my courtroom, and I'm in charge. Where was I? Oh yes, which would include another five hundred years for threatening a judge."

"You can't sentence me to thirty-two hundred years, you idiot. People only live to be about seventy years old. How the hell do you suppose that is going to happen?" Judge Marshall stood up, and so did everyone else. "Answer me, damn it. I demand an answer."

"I only wish that you could live to be that old, you murderer. I know for sure that I'll sleep better at night knowing that you won't be running around despoiling other children. That crime alone should have you put to death by, I don't know, but I know that you should suffer like no one has ever suffered before." Judge Marshall looked at her. "Mrs. Strong, I wish you the best of luck with those little girls. And even knowing that they're going to be safe with you, my heart bleeds for what has been done to them. You love them and hold them tightly, and they'll be all right, I think."

"I think so as well, sir. And thank you." He said that it had been his pleasure. "Officers, I want you to take that thing away, and I'll make arrangements for his prison term in the morning. Christ, sometimes I hate my job."

When the judge left the room, Michael was taken away as well. Once he was out of earshot, the entire courtroom burst into clapping and shouts of joy that it was finished with the Cartwrights. She only wished that she could have spoken to Mick once more before he was taken away.

~*~

Barkley was still at his desk at midnight. They'd heard from Mick so that he could thank them for his new life. It had taken Carrie nearly an hour to stop crying. It hurt him in ways that he couldn't put words to when she sobbed on his chest. Holding her and telling her that she did great was all he'd been able to do for her.

When she fell asleep on him, he was just able to slide out from under her and go check on the girls. He was also a twin, so he knew they would like it better if they were close. Putting them in the same bed had given them peace too. Almost as if they knew they had each other even if no one else did. Picking up Sunny, he kissed her on the forehead before picking up her sister. Holding them, he went to the rocker and sat down with them in his arms. He already loved these two girls so much.

"I'm going to tell you about your daddy when I think of something. While I didn't know him all that well, he was a good man and one that you should always be proud of." Rocking, he told them about the trial today and how he'd been killed. "Not really, so don't worry about that. He won't be able to come and see you anytime, not until Mr. Cartwright is dead and buried. I don't think he'll last all that long in prison anyway."

Rocking, he told them how much he loved them.

"I've only known you guys for just a few weeks, but I can't imagine a life without the two of you in it. My mom, your grandma, is so excited to babysit the two of you that she can barely contain herself. My dad too. He told me how happy he was to have little girls in the family."

Barkley thought of their biological father, Michael, and decided he wouldn't tell them about him. Not unless they asked. All he'd tell them until they were old enough to understand what he was saying. He and Carrie had agreed that they were just going to tell them that he was dead.

"I have five brothers, your uncles now, who have already decided that you two are never going to date. And if you do, they're going to be right there with you." He laughed a little. "I think it's funny, but I'd believe them if I were you. They're pretty intense about the fact that you're their nieces."

When Sunny yawned again, he joined her. Thinking that watching the two of them playing on the floor with the million and one toys they already owned was a joy that he hadn't anticipated. They were also trying to get around. Not much success at that yet, but he didn't think it would be long before they were into more things.

"Mick set the two of you up nicely. You'll be able to go to any college that you want and not have to work. Also, there will be plenty enough left over that you'll be able to buy your own home should you wish to do that. Not that I'm going to allow you out of my sight to do either of those things, but there is the help." He laughed at himself, telling two seven months old how he was going to be a helicopter parent to them. "I won't really. I mean, I'll try not to be. Perhaps when we have a couple more kids, the feeling of watching over you too much will have lessened."

He didn't think so but didn't tell them that. Looking at Bethany, she was staring at him as if she was hanging on his every word. Kissing her on the nose, she smiled at him and then continued staring.

"I have a feeling that you're going to be just like Carrie. Your mom. She's pretty intense when she's working something out. What is it that you're so frowny about?" Carrie cleared her throat at the doorway, and he smiled at her. "I was just telling them about the day we've had. I should be working, but I can't make myself do it tonight."

"You will. Even if you have to stay up all night to get it down." His grin grew. She knew him so well, he thought. He told her he'd get to it as soon as he put the girls back to bed. Carrie yawned. "Don't be too late."

As soon as the girls were down for the night, he made his way downstairs to his office and pulled up the information on the land deal again. He was so tired he could barely think. His computer had gone to sleep so many times now that he would think that it was getting a headache. He was. But he had to seriously finish the work he'd been putting off. Once he dug into it, he knew that he'd get it finished.

It was nearly three-thirty when he looked up from his computer. Barton was sitting across from him, sound asleep with his head back. He didn't snore, not really, but he did make strange noises in the back of his throat. Waking him up by just saying his name, it never ceased to amaze him that his brother could sleep like that and wake up and pick up a conversation as if there hadn't been a pause.

"I've been here for about an hour. You're boring when you work." He asked him what he wanted. Then pointed out the time to him. "I came to tell you that Michael didn't make it to prison. He was killed when he was put on the bus to take him there. Once he was seated, he grabbed the woman officer and tried to take her gun. The other officers said he kept saying how stupid and dimwitted they were for hiring a woman. She didn't have the balls to kill anyone. I guess she showed him. He was shot three times in the head, and she walked away unharmed."

"Why couldn't this wait until in the morning?" He told him what he'd heard from Mick when he'd let him know. "You know how to get in touch with him then?"

"I do. I'm to send him pictures of the girls once in a while. Also, the judge figured that I'd tell you and warned me not to tell you where he is. Mick has decided that he isn't coming back here. He said he needs to start a new life and is afraid he won't be able to do that if he is here with the girls. He also said that they'd be a sad reminder of his failure as a dad to them. I don't think he'll ever get over that feeling, but that's just me." Barkley told him he didn't think that he would either. "I thought you'd say that too. Also, you might not realize this, but you and Carrie are married."

"I know that, blockhead." Barton stood up and smiled at him. "So you're leaving because I'm married?"

"No. I'm leaving because you're a dumbass if you're down here and your pretty little wife is upstairs all by herself. I would imagine she's pinning away for someone to come to her and tell her how much she's loved and cherished. You do love and cherish her, don't you, blockhead?"

After seeing his brother out, he locked up the house and checked on the girls. Once he was sure they were safe, he made his way to the bedroom. Carrie was sound asleep and snoring softly. Undressing, he got into the bed with her, and she immediately curled her body around his. It was the best feeling he'd had in a while. Being loved and being a father.

It occurred to him in that minute that he was a father. Someone's, well, two people's dad. He nearly passed out. He was hyperventilating so hard. It wasn't until Carrie slapped him that he was able to take in a breath and let it out slowly. She asked him what the hell was wrong with him.

"I'm a dad." She glared at him. "All right, smarty pants, you're a mom too. Did that occur to you anytime tonight?"

"Yes. Several times but I didn't nearly have a heart attack while thinking about it. What would you have done had I not smacked you? Pass out and be dead to the world in the morning. What are you going to do when they start school or go on a date? Should I have an ambulance on standby for you?" Barkley told her she wasn't nice. "I'm being very nice. I didn't call you all that many names, did I?"

"They're not going to date." She stared at him hard. "They're not. I'm going to be putting my foot down on that."

"Yeah? Well, good luck with that." She rolled over with her back to him. "I'm going to tell your dad and mom what you said too. Not dating indeed. How will we ever become grandparents if they don't meet some guy and marry him."

He had to hold himself very still and not alert Carrie that he was doing it again. When she rolled over and looked at him, he tried hard to smile at her, but without breath in his lungs, he couldn't manage it. She was still making fun of him when she dumped a glass of water over his head that was on her nightstand. He could breathe again, all right, but now he was soaking wet and embarrassed. He wondered if she'd always be like this when he was having a moment. Grandparents? They were barely parents, and here she was making his a —

"Stop overthinking, Barkley and go to sleep before I have to knock your head off to get some rest. Tickling her, he nearly lost his nose when she tried to get him to stop. One thing about Carrie and being her husband, he knew that things were never going to be without fun.

Chapter 8

Carrie woke up with the sun shining in her face. Sitting up on the bed, she looked around at the messy room. Last night had been fun, she thought with a smile. Just when she was dozing off, Barkley came to the bed and jumped her bones. That's what he called it, anyway. The guy was such a romantic, she thought with a giggle.

Getting out of bed, she realized how sore she was. It wasn't from making love last night. At least she was reasonably sure about that. But who knew with that man. He could bring her to tears one moment the way he made such soft love to her. Then the next, she'd be screaming out her releases so many times that she would have a raw throat the next day. She got into the shower after turning the water on.

Her breasts had small bite marks on them. Nothing painful, just tiny bruises she thought of as badges of honor. Carrie had only asked him if he thought her breasts were too small. He'd leaned over her and took one into his mouth, laving her nipple until she nearly came before he laid back on his pillow.

"They're perfect. A mouthful for me." She asked him if he was referring to the little saying that she'd heard a long time ago. "You mean more than a mouthful is a waste? Yeah, I heard that, but honestly, I think that breasts are the most amazing part of a woman. They can bring such joy to us both. They are there for when children arrive and nurse them to keep them healthy. Did I mention how much fun they were?"

"Yes. You did." She moaned when he pulled her over him, having her sit on his groin. His cock was hard. She could feel it as it touched her. But he seemed more intent on her breasts than anything else. She watched as he cupped them both in his hands and sampled them one at a time. "That feels so amazing, Barkley."

"It does. I love how the tips peak just for me. Then when I nibble on them, they seemed to get harder still, filling my mouth with the most sensational flavors I've ever tasted." He continued to suckle at one and then the other for so long that she was sure he was never going to stop. And she didn't want him to. It felt so good to be made love to by him.

Adjusting her around so that she could slide down over his cock, she nearly came when he pressed against her clit, causing her body to tighten up to the point where she was having difficulty even breathing. He teased her about how much he was enjoying her facial expressions.

Riding Barkley — something that she'd not thought of as enjoying — she paced herself. She took her time to enjoy what she was doing and the obvious pleasure she had given to Barkley. The noises that he'd made and the look on his face were something that she'd not noticed until then. Especially the vein on his neck that was pulsing at the same rate, very quickly as his heart was.

"I love the way your skin pinks up when you're aroused." She moaned, unable to speak while her body had been in such splendor. "Your eyes are so dark right now that it's hard to believe they're usually so light. Christ, Carrie, I love you."

She had been able to come four times before he'd rolled her over onto her back. Wrapping her legs around him, for no other reason than she felt she needed to hold on, he made love to her entire body with not just his cock but his hands, mouth and legs.

Each stroke of his hand down her body sent shivers over her. Carrie felt the goosebumps rise on her flesh. It had been sexy in the most wonderful way. Simply the way her body responded to his touch was something that she was sure she'd never get enough of.

His legs slid up and down hers. Reaching down to his ass, she cupped her hands on his muscled flesh and nearly came when he moved in a way that had him touching her clit. It wasn't enough yet, too much at the same time.

Her breasts were tender from what he'd done to her last night. He'd not hurt her, no, never that, but he continued to taste her nipples, suckling on her breasts. Even thinking about it now had her cupping her breasts to feel the pleasure once again.

Getting out of the shower, she thought about when they'd come together. He had held her to him, kissing her so wonderfully tender that she came twice while his tongue explored parts of her mouth that she'd not felt before. When he tightened his grip on her, holding her to her while he fucked her harder, Carrie saw stars when her body let go.

Holding onto the sink while her body went through the same climax as last night, she was dizzy with the thrill of it. Her body was stiff with it. Sitting down on the commode, she held onto the sink while her body adjusted. Christ, she'd never in her life had come without a man. It was a heady feeling and one that she thought Barkley might enjoy some time.

Carrie was getting dressed when her phone rang. She was still lightheaded from the climax, but she was moving around better. Picking up the phone, the number was unknown to her, so she decided not to answer it. Putting the phone back, she finished getting dressed, fixed her hair and made her way to the kitchen, where she could hear her daughters — such a wonderful sound — were having their breakfast. She found all of her family there, as well as their spouses.

Since they didn't notice her coming into the room and were getting louder by the second, she did something she'd been known to do to get the attention of people who weren't paying attention to her. She put her fingers into her mouth and let go of a whistle surpassing anything she'd ever done before.

Sitting down at the table in the dining room, they all followed. Her nephews, Neal and Paula's children, came to sit on her lap while Robert and Dan brought the high chairs in with the girls still in them. They seemed to be delighted to be moved around like that. Carrie asked what was going on. She smiled at Donna, Aaron's wife, when she raised her hand. Forever a teacher, that one.

"We've been discussing jobs here. I think it's a given that you'll be staying here now that you're married, and there isn't any way that any of us want to live so far away from you and Barkley. Who, you might want to know, is our favorite person for agreeing to marry you." She thanked Donna. "You're welcome. There are plenty of houses around. A few might need a little work, but you know us. We're willing to do some extra to have a nice home."

"Dan and I went to look at the house on Fifth yesterday. After thinking about it on the way home, we decided it was much too small for what we had in mind. It's only two bedrooms, and if everyone is going to be living here, we'll need extra room when our nieces and nephews want to come and visit us." Barkley walked into the room with his parents. After kissing her on the mouth and then the girls, Robert continued. "As you know, I can work from anywhere with my job. But Dan is going to need to find a restaurant that will be willing to take him on as head chef."

"I have just the place for you on that, Dan. There used to be a restaurant in town called the Mill. It's long since been closed down. It'll need a full upgrade and cleaning, but it would be great to have someone running it that cooks as well as you do. Also, since we own the building and the land, we'll help you get it up to par so long as you hire locally for the construction as well as workers." Dan said that he could do that. "Great. One less thing that we have to worry about. As a foundation, we are trying to bring more work to this area, and while you won't hire thousands of people to work there, it will be a beginning."

She watched as Barkley senior handed a file to her brother. As they went over it, he pulled out another file and handed it over to Neal and Paula. Neal had been in construction since he'd been sixteen. He'd worked himself up to be a foreman but never to the point where he owned one himself. Barkley told him of his plan.

"We could use a good construction company around here. Not just for building and remodeling but also to do things like yard work for some of the downtown buildings that need it. I know for a fact that the city had turned that over to local men, but they lack organization in getting anything done. What do you say about running it for us? The same thing applies to this job. Buy locally when you can, as well as hire as many locals as you can." Neal told him he'd not been anything but a foreman before. "Yes, but when I researched the firm that you worked with, they told me that most of the time, it's you in charge when the owner is out or too hungover to come to work."

After going over some of the things that needed to be started right away, Neal turned to Aaron and asked him if he'd partner with him. Aaron had a degree in landscaping, and with the permission and excitement of Barkley, they were going to set the town on their ears, they told him.

"I don't know that the town can handle that, but I'm glad that you can get this started for us. It's something that has needed to be done for some time now, and I'm happy to know that it will be in good hands." Neal asked about equipment. "As it just so happens, there is a large auction on Monday of a construction/landscaping company that has gone under. For no other reason than the man's family didn't run it correctly, and it couldn't survive. If you're willing, the three of us, and anyone else that wishes to go, will hit that early in the morning and see about getting things for us."

Andrew and CarolAnn were going to work for the foundation. Both of them were certified accountants, and the Strong Foundation needed extra hands in that area to keep things and money rolling in. Carrie looked around at her family and realized that in the hour that Barkley and his parents had shown up, each of her brothers had a good job, one that they would love.

When everyone turned to her, she told them she had a job. It was Barkley that laughed. Asking him what that was supposed to mean, he leaned back and pointed to his mother. She apparently had big plans for her.

"I do really have a job." Lisa asked her if she liked it or even enjoyed it. "Not particularly. But it pays... paid the bills."

"I have a job for you that will have you working with me. I run a few charities that I'm going to have to walk away from, and I'd like to have you take them over." She asked her why she was walking away. "Nothing nefarious. I just want to have more time to spend with the grandchildren that are coming along, and I thought that if you took them over, I'd be able to watch the children more. All of your children."

They all talked about the jobs, and then Lisa told them of the houses the foundation owned that they could have first dibs on. Most of them were larger homes made for families with children. Carrie thought that would be perfect for her brothers and families as they all had children but Robert. He, however, seemed content to be the greatest uncle of all times.

"Since it's still early, I thought that we could go and look at them and get you situated in them soon. I know you'll all need to have your things back home packed up. That's a given. But we can help you with that too." Barkley looked at her. "I want my new family to be happy here so Carrie can be happy with you all here."

"Dan and I aren't going back. We might decide to have someone pack us up, but we've no desire to go there again." Carrie had heard about the signs and was as pissed off as they were about it. "If you could arrange for someone you trust, Barkley, to go in and do that for us, we'd be indebted to you for the rest of our lives."

"Consider it done. And if you'd like to make it known that you're not going to be putting up with their shit again, just let me know. I cannot stand people that have a hard time with others that are different than they are." Dan was nearly brought to tears and left them there, only to return a few minutes later with a tin of cookies that he said he'd baked just yesterday. "You're a good man, Dan. But if I spend too much time around you, I'm going to be either severely overweight or a diabetic. These are fantastic." Just the words they needed to bring the room back to being in a good mood.

After getting the girls ready in some of their new outfits and figuring out the stroller, they all walked to the house instead of driving. It was a beautiful day for walking as spring was just coming around, and the weather was warm enough for them to be out. Lisa suggested dinner after they were finished, and everyone agreed. These families were going to be doing a great many things together and making things happen not just for her family but the town as well. She could almost see it happening as they walked around the town, pointing out things that needed to be looked into.

~*~

Barton moved along the line of products that were being made by the company. He'd only been here for three days, and he'd yet to put his finger on why the place wasn't making more money than they were. He made his way to his office, one that he was using temporarily while he was here.

No one knew who he was other than a manager that had only been just hired by the company. Not even the owners of the company were aware that he was the one that was going to decide whether or not they got the money that they so desperately needed. It was at the point where they expanded or went under. But without finding the source of their issues, there was no way that he was going to recommend helping them out. Something fishy was going on, as his grannie said all the time.

"Mr. Lemon?" He nearly forgot his alias and looked up at the woman in front of him. "There is a person at the front gate that says they're here for inspection of the lines in the kitchen. Something about them being graded?"

He had no idea but nodded to her and followed her to the front office. As soon as the woman in question walked in, he had to think for a moment about where he knew her from. It was Tessa Brown. Christ, this was all he needed.

"Do I—" He cut her off, telling her his name was Burt Lemon. "Yes, of course. I'm the inspector for the state. I was sent here to look over the lines and make sure that they're up to code."

She looked as confused as he was. Seriously?

Today of all days. He asked if he could guide her to the kitchen area, and she agreed. Somewhat hesitantly, but she was playing along for now, and he was glad for that. As soon as the other woman left him, Tessa started walking alongside him.

"I'm assuming you have a good reason for being Mr. Lemon and not Mr. Strong." Her voice was low and filled with a great deal of humor. "Not that you don't look like a lemon right now, but I'm genuinely surprised to see you here."

"As I am you. I'm here to see why this company is losing money hand over fist. It's easier for me to come here undercover than to show up as Mr. Barton Strong, money lender." She nodded, and they opened the door to the kitchen. "Christ."

To say that both of them were surprised by what they walked in on would have been grossly understated. Not only were the employees smoking while baking the small cakes that had made the place famous years ago, but they weren't wearing the proper attire, no gloves, masks or even shoes on a couple of them.

"Mr. Lemon, is this normal for this place?" He

said he'd not made it to the kitchen as yet as the people stopped working just long enough to look to see who was coming in and blow them off. With her voice even lower than before, this time, it wasn't filled with humor but anger. He was sure it was only topped by his own anger by a few degrees. "I'm going to have to shut this place down. Right now."

He nodded and walked around the kitchen with her. No one stopped them or even bothered to hide what they were doing wrong. Barton watched ash from one of the worker's cigarette drop into the pan he was currently filling with batter. It nearly made him sick to know he'd had one of these cakes just this morning.

He kept an eye on Tessa as she told the workers to stop what they were doing and to back away from what they were doing. Not one of the twenty or so people in the room moved, not even when she threatened to call the police. The man who had dropped the ash told her that they had a deadline and they had it hit it or not get paid. Pulling out her phone, she called for backup, she called it. The police, she told the people were on their way. Barton called Trevor. He was the one that had sent him here.

"The police have been called in. This is a mess, Trev. Not only are they smoking, but two of the people are barefooted. When asked why, they said that they worked better that way. I'm about to puke my guts up. This is so nasty." He asked if he thought that was why they were losing money. "If I were to hazard a guess, I'd say this is the main reason for the returns he was telling us about. Also, the loss of a great many stores. I wouldn't buy one of these cakes if it was the only morsel of food left in the world."

"I had no idea that Tessa was a food service inspector, did you?" Barton told her younger brother that had he known, he might have called her in himself. "Yes, me too. I'm guessing you'd not made it in the kitchen until now. Why?"

"We, as you know, thought that it was the lines that were screwing up orders. This is the reason for a lot of the feedback we got from not just store owners but the customer baseline as well." He had to get out of the kitchen while the idiots were still doing their job. "They act like this is an everyday occurrence, Trev. Do you suppose that someone is paying off the inspectors that come in here usually?" He'd not thought to ask

Tessa if this was her regular route but did so when she came out. She told him, and then he relayed it to his brother. "Tessa is here because the one that usually comes here is in the hospital. She said she picked up four of his places while the rest had been distributed to other inspectors. I think that someone needs to hit the other places with a police escort. This place is — oh holy Christ, Trevor. I just saw a rat the size of that cat we used to have as children. I'm going to recommend that this place be condemned right now. Oh, I'm going to be sick."

Passing his phone off to Tessa, he ran to the closest trash can and emptied his stomach. He was sick with the thought that he'd eaten several of the cakes over the last few days, trying to decide if he liked them or not. He most assuredly wasn't ever going to like them or perhaps cake again. When he felt his belly was empty, he sat down on the cool floor just as the police arrived.

"Are you all right?" He told Tessa he wasn't sure. "Yeah, I can understand that. You ate some of them —"

"Don't say it." She giggled, and for whatever reason, it made him less grumpy about being sick.

"What happens now? I mean, you must know that this place is going to close up and never reopen again."

"The place will be inspected from top to bottom, and then after the rating is put in place, it will be up to the owners of the building to decide what course of action they want to go with." She looked at him with a cocked brow. "Do you guys own this place? I mean, it's a little out of your zone, isn't it? Being in another state."

"We own the land, not the building. I know that sounds weird, but that's about all our involvement in what they produce here. But I'm going to recommend to Dad and the others that they tear it down." He told her about the rat. "I swear to you, it was as big as a full-grown cat."

"More than likely. If you see one, you can bet your sweet ass there are more." She didn't seem the least bit upset about what had happened. He asked her about it. "You sort of get jaded after a while. I mean, I sort of like my job, but more often than not, I see this sort of thing too much."

"Don't tell me where. I want to remain blissfully unaware." She told him that, more than likely, he didn't want to know. Tessa also told him that most of the public didn't either. "I can well imagine."

He looked around as the people in the kitchen were brought out in cuffs. Barton didn't understand why they were being arrested, but he didn't ask. The less he knew what was going on in the kitchen right now, the better he'd feel. Standing up, he went to the fountain to get some water and decided against it. Looking at Tessa, he asked her what she was going to do now that the place was closed up.

"A team will come in tomorrow and go over the entire building. The kitchen won't be the only place that is in violation of codes. Then after that, it'll be determined, as I said, if they're shut down forever or not." She handed him his phone. "Your brother said he'd talk to you later. He was going to get with the others to make decisions about the land. He asked me my opinion. No one has ever done that before with me."

"Trevor is like that. He will gather up as much information as he can before he makes any kind of decision." He watched as the police started going around the building to get the rest of the employees out. "Do you know of a good place where we can get a good meal? I'm suddenly hungry."

"My place. If you want clean food." He said he did and followed her out the door when they were asked to leave. "I didn't drive here. So can we ride to my home together? I was dropped off by my mom. She was going to pick me up later and take me home."

"Yes, of course. How is your mom?" Tessa told him she was doing much better now that she was working with a specialist about her belly issues. "Mom told me that she'd found someone to help her out. It must be taxing to have an illness for that long, and no one has helped out with it."

"More so than you can imagine. She's a wonderful person, but when she's in pain, it hurts me to the point where I want to pull out a gun and make them find out what is wrong. But this doctor that she's seeing, he's been running his own tests since we got home. I think she's just happy that someone cares enough now." They were in the car and putting on their seat belts when her phone rang. After asking her if she wanted him to give her privacy, she told him it was her mom. She put it on speaker and told her briefly what had happened. "I'm leaving now. Barton Strong was here when I got here, working undercover. We're going to my house for some food. What to join us?"

"Oh, that would be lovely, but I have a meeting with the women's league tonight. I haven't any idea why they call it that. It's just a bunch of old women fussing about how things aren't getting done as quickly as we'd hope they would. No, you two have a nice dinner, and I'll see you in the morning. We're still on for breakfast at my place, correct?" Tessa told her mom that they were still on. "All right, Darling. I'll see you then. Have a good time, Barton."

"I will, Mrs. Brown." As they left the parking lot, Barton saw that the police were putting someone at the gate. Also, he'd noticed that they'd put chains on the doors as well as had an officer at each exit of the building. "Do you need anything for us to pick up? Any kind of food?"

"No. I have it all at home. Unless you would like a bottle of wine. I have a couple of bottles left from New Year's, but there is a reason that I've not polished them off yet." He said that he'd see about finding a place to get some. "I know of a place that sells good wines and bad ones. If you don't mind, we'll head there first."

He was game and told her so. As soon as they pulled up in front of the small building, he knew that he was going to have to make a trip here with his brothers sometimes. The Wine and Cheesery wasn't the only specialty place on the street.

He was glad that she'd suggested this place when he left with not just a bottle of wine for dinner but four bottles that he was taking home for himself. They'd also gotten a cheese and meat platter to have while they were there. It was just the kind of place that he loved to find, just for something different.

"They have olives as well. I'm not a big fan of black olives, but I can eat anything else they have. My favorite is the ones that have stuffing in them." He ordered a small plate of them, too, so they could try them. Tessa was a great tour guide, and they ended up having dinner in one of her favorite places. The Regency Hotel.

When asked, he told her to order for him. There was very little that he didn't like, and Barton was a huge lover of trying new things. When their salad arrived, she pointed out the different items on it. He thought his favorite was the onions that had been pickled.

"They make their own croutons here too. As well as a lot of the breakfast items. Sometimes when I'm feeling a little sorry for myself, I stay the night in the hotel just so I can be pampered a little. It's about the most fun I allow myself." She laughed when he did. "This hotel has been here forever, I guess. Recently they have updated the rooms but left the splendor of the nineteen thirties too. There are even rooms that have dumbwaiters in the rooms for those who like to dine in their rooms."

When they left, both of them stuffed and sated, he asked her what she wanted for dessert. As they passed an ice cream shop, she told him that she'd never been in the shop before. They both ended up with a dish of three different kinds of the treat, sharing it while they sat outside on the chairs and tables that had been provided. He asked her about herself.

"Nothing much to tell. I'm an inspector. I've had a good life, mostly thanks to my grandparents and mom. When my father died or was killed by my uncle, I guess, it was just myself and Mom for a long time. Grandma came to stay with us when my step-grandda died, and we had some good times." He asked her if she had a steady boyfriend. "I don't have one. Do you want that title, Mr. Strong? I mean, we've spent an enjoyable evening together. Should we become an item?"

Instead of answering her, he leaned over and kissed her. It was only meant to be a quick peck on the lips, but as soon as his mouth touched hers, he wanted more. When he pulled back, or she did, he wasn't sure. Barton thought about all the things that he wanted to do with her. None of them were for the public view.

"I'm not easy." He said that he never thought she was. "Good. But I am going to ask you back to my place or your hotel where we can take up where the kiss left off. No strings attached, but I would like to have sex with you."

He nearly raced her to his car. As they we pulling up in front of her home, Barton nearly asked her if she was sure about this. But as soon as she undid her seatbelt, she came and sat on his lap. Barton hoped they made it indoors before he took her on his front seat.

Before You Go...

HELP AN AUTHOR

write a review

THANK YOU!

Share your voice and help guide other readers to these wonderful books. Even if it's only a line or two, your reviews help readers discover the author's books so they can continue creating stories that you'll love. Log in to your favorite retailer and leave a review. Thank you.

Kathi Barton, a winner of the Pinnacle Book Achievement Award and a best-selling author on Amazon and All Romance books, lives in Nashport, Ohio, with her husband, Paul. When not creating new worlds and romance, Kathi and her husband enjoy camping and going to auctions. She can also be seen at county fairs with her husband, an artist and potter.

Her muse, a cross between Jimmy Stewart and Hugh Jackman, brings her stories to life for her readers in a way that has them coming back time and again for more. Her favorite genre is paranormal romance, with a great deal of spice. You can visit Kathi online and drop her an email if you'd like. She loves hearing from her fans. aaronskiss@gmail.com.

Follow Kathi on her blog: http://kathisbartonauthor.blogspot.com/

www.ingramcontent.com/pod-product-compliance
Lightning Source LLC
Chambersburg PA
CBHW030222180626
46810CB00008B/2927